Fr ... ure—a rej ... that suddenly goes ... . . . a universe that turns into a chessboard of nightmares . . . a strange love in an alien world . . . a ghoulish planet that drives men mad . . . the arrival of the terrifying supermen of tomorrow . . .

NEW WRITINGS IN S.F.—1

Five science fiction stories
edited by John Carnell

Also edited by JOHN CARNELL

NEW WRITINGS IN S.F.—2
NEW WRITINGS IN S.F.—3
NEW WRITINGS IN S.F.—4
NEW WRITINGS IN S.F.—5
NEW WRITINGS IN S.F.—6
NEW WRITINGS IN S.F.—7
NEW WRITINGS IN S.F.—8
NEW WRITINGS IN S.F.—9
NEW WRITINGS IN S.F.—10
NEW WRITINGS IN S.F.—11
NEW WRITINGS IN S.F.—12
NEW WRITINGS IN S.F.—13
NEW WRITINGS IN S.F.—14
NEW WRITINGS IN S.F.—15
NEW WRITINGS IN S.F.—16

and published by CORGI BOOKS

Edited by John Carnell

New Writings in S.F.—1

TRANSWORLD PUBLISHERS LTD
A National General Company

NEW WRITINGS IN S.F.—1

A CORGI BOOK 552 08411 5

Originally published in Great Britain
by Dobson Books, Ltd.

PRINTING HISTORY
Dobson Books Edition published 1964
Corgi Edition published 1964
Corgi Edition reprinted 1965
Corgi Edition reissued 1970

All the characters in this book are fictitious and any resemblance to actual persons, living or dead, is purely coincidental.

Corgi Books are published by Transworld Publishers, Ltd., Bashley Road, London, N.W.10

Made and printed in Great Britain by
Richard Clay (The Chaucer Press), Ltd., Bungay, Suffolk

CONTENTS

FOREWORD

NEW WRITINGS IN S-F is a radical departure in the field of the science fiction short story. As its name implies, not only *new* stories written specially for the series as well as s-f stories which would not normally be seen by the vast majority of readers, will appear in future editions, but *new* styles, ideas, and even *new* writers who have something worth contributing to the *genre*, will be presented.

For nearly forty years the science fiction short story has been the main platform from which this fascinating literary medium developed. Almost all its leading authors—Aldiss, Asimov, Ballard, Bradbury, Clarke, Harrison, Pohl, Russell, Simak, Sturgeon, Tenn, Wyndham, and many others—first contributed to the s-f short story before writing their first novels. Without the specialized magazines in which these short stories originally appeared, there would be little or no background to science fiction today and it would probably languish in the "speculative romance" of the H. G. Wells era. In recent years, however, the specialized magazines have only had a limited appeal, primarily to a male audience either technically trained or technically minded. It was left to the expanding hardcover publishing field and the mass market of the paperback to introduce this exciting medium to a vaster general public already conscious that Man was on the threshold of space travel. In this respect, its many editors were forced to select material from the best stories *already* published and familiar to the *aficionados*.

Now the time has come to take this development one natural stage further—and introduce *new* material specially written and selected for the *new* market.

This first volume of *New Writings in S-F* is but a brief sample of the many and varied excursions into the Realm of Perhaps we shall be taking in future months, for science fiction covers a tremendously wide field—apart from all the sciences, it also deals with sociology, psychology, medicine, politics, genetics, and even religion, and embraces such long-term speculations as telepathy, time travel, faster-than-light journies, and a host of other improbable probabilities.

As a cross-section of the many things to come, *New Writings in S-F No. 1* tackles several themes from different angles. Edward Mackin's satirical "Key to Chaos" points out that science does not always know where it is going and that often a bumbling mistake can be turned to advantage. Brian W. Aldiss's grim little vignette, "Man on Bridge", indicates that Man himself is but a small creature in the Cosmos and that his meddlings, especially with himself, could well produce a monster (in more ways than one) than an ideal superman.

In the present everyday world of expanding birthrate and the overwhelming problem of feeding the vast horde now literally crawling across the face of the planet, expansion to the planets and even the stars is often uppermost in the minds of many s-f writers, and three of the contributors to this volume have tackled the idea from completely different viewpoints. Damien Broderick, an interesting new Australian writer, shows in "To the Sea's Furthest End" that the same problem facing Earth today could well apply when Man has expanded throughout the galaxy, while American authors Joseph Green and James Webbert, in their joint effort "Haggard Honeymoon", brilliantly point out the fact that alien worlds will have an alien environment and that Man will have to adapt to survive. "Two's Company", by John Rankine, shows yet another facet of the same problem, but with the emphasis on the individual effort so necessary to overcome a specific problem—in this case, survival.

Science fiction (an unwieldy and unattractive title which should more aptly be called "Speculative fiction") is now expanding into the field of general literature and has largely outstripped the western romance in popularity and is fast catching up with the thriller. *New Writings in S-F* will, in future volumes, form a bridgehead between the old and new versions of speculative fiction.

We hope that you enjoy the journey.

John Carnell

May 1964

KEY TO CHAOS

by

EDWARD MACKIN

Humour in science fiction is one of the rarest commodities and probably the most difficult to write. However, Edward Mackin, a well-known author in this medium, successfully bridges the gap between seriousness and levity in describing the adventures of an inventor and a cyberneticist when they produce a rejuvenating machine.

KEY TO CHAOS

THE first time I met Frank Tetchum he was hammering on the front door of an apartment house block on East Third Level. Beside him was a chair, a small table, and a plastic bowl with some cutlery in it. Evicted tenants are not an uncommon sight in these parts, and I was about to walk on when he spoke to me.

"It's one thing being slung out," he said heatedly, "but it's a bit thick when they slap an order on your furniture and you don't even owe any rent. The scoundrels have got my id-scope in there, too, and they're hanging on to it." He recommenced his hammering on the door, using the chair this time.

I looked at him, curiously. He was slimly built, perhaps thirty years old, and badly in need of a shave. "What's an id-scope?" I asked.

He put the chair down, and frowned at me. "It's a thought visualizer," he said. "I invented it." Then he went back to his frenzied assault on the door, and smashed the chair without eliciting any response.

I tapped him on the shoulder. "Every citizen should know his rights," I told him. "You are entitled to the tools of your trade and any items under contract or order if you haven't been bankrupted by due process of law. Have you?"

He dropped the splintered chair and shook his head. "I don't think so," he said. "I'd have known about it, wouldn't I?"

"You'd have known about it," I agreed. "It's a kind of legal sausage machine. Once you've been through it you know exactly how much skin you fill, and it's always less than you thought. Anyhow, just leave this to me. I'll fix it for you." I placed my mouth against the communicator near the door. "This man is entitled to his invention!" I bellowed. "He is under contract to supply it to the Government."

The door was wrenched open immediately, and I found myself looking at a character who had to bend at the waist to get his ugly face through the doorway. I estimated that he wasn't quite as big as both of us put together.

"You want somethin'?" he asked. "Like maybe a dismantling job, starting with your head?"

"I believe this gentleman would like a word with you," I said quickly, taking a step back.

Politeness costs nothing. I took another step back in case he thought I was crowding him, and somehow found myself behind the inventor; but, after all, it was his problem, not mine. In any case, no one will deny that inventors are probably the most expendable members of the community. If there's one thing this jaded cul-de-sac of an age needs least it's another invention, suffering as it does from a kind of mal-de-mechanism.

"I want my id-scope," the inventor told him, simply.

The big boy turned to someone behind him. "You hear that, Ben?" he said, grinning. "He wants his id-scope."

Another man squeezed into the doorway, and I was slightly relieved to note that he was nearer my own height and weight.

"Ain't that most unfortunate," he said, showing his ugly fangs in what he probably thought was a smile. "It just so happens that I haven't no knowledge of what an id-scope might be. How about you, Pete?"

The big fellow shook his head slowly from side to side in mock mystification. "Me too," he said. "As far as I'm concerned all we got in here is furniture. I wouldn't know an id-scope if I fell over it. Is there anything else you'd like?"

With great temerity the inventor put an end to the baiting by poking his finger into the giant's chest. "You get back up your beanstalk," he snarled. "I'd rather deal with your mate."

A hand swept out and the inventor was hefted off the ground. The bailiff brought him to eye-level, and delivered his piece. "Listen, Jack," he said. "Any more of the old acid and you get trodden on." He dropped the startled inventor, who took a couple of stumbling steps backwards and then fell over. "Do yourself a favour and beat it," the bailiff advised. The door was closed with the kind of force that has the emphasis of finality.

I helped him to his feet. "Hard luck," I commiserated. "You've drawn a couple of dillies there, all right. Someone meant to make it stick."

"Hard luck?" he echoed. "You don't know the half of it. I had a firm offer only this morning from Benson Industries. Old Benson himself came to see me yesterday and had a look at the id-scope. He videoed an offer of three thousand this morning; but I held out for more."

"My poor friend," I said, "I've got news for you. I happen to know that Julius Benson owns this apartment block. You should have accepted the offer."

Tears welled up in his eyes. "The swine!" he said. "How could anyone be so unscrupulous?"

"With Julius it comes easy. He's had loads of practice. Just the same, that id thing of yours must be a credit-dazzler if dear Julius thinks it's got what it takes to line up the lemons."

"Yes, well, I was putting another nought on it myself," he told me, rather diffidently.

I shook my head. "I know Benson, and I can tell you that you're still selling short. There must be enough money in that thing to tilt a bank."

Taking time out to think about it myself I warmed towards the unfortunate inventor. Perhaps there are too many inventors around these days; but this appeared to be a particularly useful invention. A useful invention being one that can hit the jackpot all over, especially when I am around to help collect.

I took him by the arm. "Men like you," I said earnestly, "are the salt of the earth, and I am not going to stand by and see you defrauded, gypped, or otherwise flim-flammed. We are going to get that wonderful invention of yours back, whatever the devil it is, and we are going to squeeze Benson till his eyes pop out and bounce off his cheque book. I want nothing for myself, of course. I just like to see justice done."

"No, that won't do," he protested. "You really must have something for your trouble. If we get the id-scope back I'll cut you in for ten per cent."

"Twenty-five," I said quickly. "I have to cover expenses."

He seemed surprised. "But I thought you said . . . Oh, all right. Twenty-five it is." He thrust out his hand. "My name is Frank Tetchum."

"Mine is Hek Belov," I told him, and we shook hands. "This is going to be a very lucrative partnership. I can feel it in my bones. My friend, you are very fortunate that I happened to come along when I did. It means that your troubles are practically over."

"How do we get the id-scope back?" he wanted to know. "That's the first thing. Have you any ideas?"

I had, but when I examined them closer they appeared to be chiefly concerned with food or the occasional almost unbosomed doxy passing with a young cav, wearing an enormous Stuart hat, a balloon jacket with frilled cuffs, and carrying a loaded stick, which he would use given the slightest opportunity. But we all suffer to a greater or lesser extent from this sort of poor signal-to-noise ratio, and how else could it be when the world is so much with us?

My continuing poverty, too, places a constant strain on my thought processes. I find that I think better with a little security. You'd imagine that a cyberneticist of my capabilities would have that; but what with the increase in self-repair machinery and production lines, the average cyberneticist finds it very difficult to make even a bare living, and a genius like myself, if I may say so, is frozen out completely. Why? Possibly because he refuses to be a yessiring, lickspittling, nut-and-bolter. The fact that I have no recognized qualifications has nothing to do with it. You could drive a heavy haulage truck through a PY computer, and I'll guarantee to have it working again within a week. That's the kind of cyberneticist I am.

I closed my eyes to concentrate on our immediate problem, and it came to me like a flash. "I've solved it, I think," I said, jubilantly. "How much money do you have?"

He dug into his pocket and produced a handful of coins. "That much," he said.

"We'll have to cut back on part of the scheme then, like fifty credits worth, and take a few more chances. Come on. We've a video call to make."

I videoed the nearest hover trucking company and told the clerk that I was Mr. Julius Benson of Benson Industries. It was possible that he might know Benson by sight, or had seen a picture of him, so I had thoughtfully squeezed a piece of crumpled cellophane into the scanner-lens hood. It also disguised the fact that I wasn't sitting in an office, and using a private line.

He mentioned the poor definition; but I ignored this, and explained that I wanted someone to pick up a fairly heavy piece of scientific equipment from an address on East Third Level. I gave him Frank Tetchum's address, and said I wanted the equipment taking to Benson House where there would be a couple of men ready to unload it.

"Just tell the bailiffs that Mr. Benson requires the id-scope right away," I explained. "They'll give your man a hand with it."

"A special shipping of this nature comes rather expensive, sir," he said. "It would be about three times the usual rates. Of course, if you'd like to wait for our regular run-around we could probably fix you up in a couple of days' time."

"I don't care what it costs, you idiot!" I shouted. "I want it shipping immediately. Is that understood?"

"Yes, sir," he said, fawning. "Of course, sir."

He'd slam another ten per cent on for that insult. I certainly hoped so, because he'd be billing Benson, and not me; but I was willing to bet that they'd never collect, anyway.

"I don't get it," Tetchum said, when we came out of the video box. "Where do we get the money from to pay the truckers? And why deliver it to Benson's place?" He frowned. "Just a minute," he said, with a deepening suspicion in his tone. "Whose side are you on? You're not working for Benson, are you?"

I glared at him. "All right, then," I said. "I throw my hand in. I'm not beating my brains out over your problems only to be accused of treachery. It isn't worth it for a mere thirty per cent."

"Twenty-five was the figure we agreed on," he reminded me.

"I don't hear so good," I said. "Did you say thirty-five per cent? I really couldn't put my unique talents at your disposal for less than that."

"All right," he sighed, "thirty-five it is; but that's the top limit, and I'm trusting you because I've got no alternative."

"Thank you for the vote of confidence," I gritted, clicking my teeth at him. "The next move is to get to Benson House and hang about there till that truck shows up."

When it arrived, which was about half-an-hour after we got there, the driver proved to be a tired, middle-aged man with a distinct aversion to lifting anything except his big, flat feet.

"You want to take it easy," I told him. "Just leave this thing to us. We can manage."

He nodded, disinterestedly, and produced the consignment notes. I scribbled a spurious signature across the top copy, and he tore off the flimsy and gave it to me.

"That'll be thirty-nine credits," he said. "Where do I collect?"

"The cashier's office," I directed. "Third floor; but you'll have to walk. The lift's out of order."

It had been out of order ever since I'd removed the fuses.

He swore; but without any enthusiasm. "Aren't they always?" he said, tiredly, and proceeded to make the long climb to disillusionment.

The id-scope looked a bit like one of those pic-flips of what-the-butler-saw vintage. I was pleased to see that it was on wheels, because it was bigger than I'd expected. Tetchum patted it affectionately.

"Am I pleased to see you!" he said happily.

"Save the reunion speech," I told him. "We're not out of the wood yet."

We wheeled the thing down the short ramp, took it at speed through Benson House, and down the baggage lift to First Level.

"Where are we going?" Tetchum wanted to know.

"About three hundred yards along to the right there's a deserted office building. It's been condemned for years; but it will do for a hidey-hole."

He shook his head. "I hope you know what you're doing, that's all," he said. "I just hope you know what you're doing."

I forebore to reply. I knew what I was doing all right. As

soon as we could get this thing stashed away somewhere in the building I was going to video Benson, and gauge how much interest he had in the machine. But first I had to see what it could do myself. Up to now I had been playing along on what was little more than a hunch. What Tetchum had given me could have been a load of poppycock, only I didn't think so.

"By heavens!" I exclaimed involuntarily. "I must be desperate for money!"

I was, too.

It was easy enough getting into the building. The main door had disappeared and had been replaced by a sheet of plasteel, which in its turn had been wrenched away, and hung by one corner. Finding a room that was fairly secure was a bit more difficult. It had to be on the ground floor because there was no lift.

We finally opted for what had once been the washroom. I noticed a tarnished brass key on the floor among the bits of debris from the ceiling. After I had cleaned it up I found that, with a bit of coaxing, it worked the lock.

"We're in business," I said. "Put the thing through its paces. I want to see if it was worth it."

"How can I?" asked Tetchum. "There's no juice."

"There soon will be," I promised. I located the incoming supply cable, broke the Company's seal, and hooked up to the board with a bit of wire cut from a section of the lighting circuit. "Connect up," I told him.

He found a power socket and shoved the plug in. Then he switched on, and gazed through the oval lens, adjusting various controls.

"That's it," he said at last, with a pleased smile. "She's nicely warmed up. But first of all I'd better explain how it works, and what you can expect to see."

"Keep it brief," I warned. "We've got to work fast from now on because of the risk of detection."

He slid a panel back at the base of the machine and pulled out a kind of skull-cap arrangement. "This is the cerebrator pickup," he explained. "The anodes press against your skull, something after the fashion of an encephalograph, and the variations in the brain rhythm are converted into magnetic impulses. These are fed to the id-scope amplifier. The viewing part of the scope consists of a three-inch layer of fine iron dust enclosed in a globular electro-matrix, which has a viewing slot. The electro-matrix is actually built up of thousands of tiny, powerful electro-magnets, and these are influenced by the variations in the brain rhythms of the viewer. These control and shape the iron dust.

"The real heart of the machine is the translator; but I won't go into that. It translates the brain rhythms into picture forms, by a process of surface rejection, breaking the whole thing down to what I call the K-line. This feeds into the magnets and the result is that the iron dust provides a solid image, coloured in by the same K-line variations fed into a more or less normal projector."

"Marvellous," I said, clicking my teeth at him. "What next! Does it make good coffee, too?" He seemed nonplussed. "Get on with it," I told him. "You're not in the Academy of Applied Sciences here. Just give me the bare bones."

That's another thing about inventors. They talk too much.

"Well," he continued uncertainly, "if that's the way you want it, I'll just add that you'll be able to see your innermost thoughts, ambitions, and desires presented solidly before your eyes. A tape record of the whole thing is made automatically and can be fed back any time so that anyone can see the other man's id-wish."

It was just another peep-show, and I saw no future for it. "Couldn't you have invented a better can-opener instead?" I asked him. "I can't see what's in it for Benson. Are you sure he made you an offer?"

He nodded, and almost smirked. "He made it all right. Just look for yourself, and maybe you'll see why." He offered me the contact pickup. "Here, put it on."

I took it from him, and put my pocket Simmons across the output flex to satisfy myself that there wasn't something lethal waiting to pounce upon my unique cerebrum. Satisfied, I put it on.

"I'll bet you look under the bed," Tetchum remarked sarcastically.

"I always sleep on the floor," I told him. "I can't stand heights."

He adjusted the controls again, and I watched the tiny, global arena light up. There was a swirl of dust that suddenly became a recognizable scene, and I gazed almost open-mouthed at what followed. If this was my secret id-wish then I should have been born into a sultanship or something of the kind. At least I had a nice taste in women; but I wasn't prepared to accept that I was a lecher and a glutton. In fact, I had always prided myself on being a gentleman, and a gourmet. It came as a shock to see myself squatting on a throne of gold and tearing at what looked like half a sheep, with the grease running down my chin, while a dozen girls swarmed around me dressed in diaphanous garments that left little to the imagination.

I took the skull-cap pickup off and turned to Tetchum. "Very interesting," I said, "you insulting swine!"

"Don't get so upset," he grinned. "You should have seen Benson's." He pressed a button marked *Repeat*, and looked into the lens. Then he glanced at the meters on the control panel. "Slight over-bias," he said. "I should have adjusted that. Still, not to worry. Yours is a quite normal sort of id-wish. You must remember that the id is an untamed savage. I think yours came out of it very well. I'm sorry I can't show you Benson's. He had me wipe it off the tape. Part of it was where he was smashing up the Elgin Marbles with a fifty-six pound sledge-hammer while it rained gold pieces. The rest was even crazier. His id is probably mad."

"And what about yours?" I asked.

"I'll switch it through for you," he said, and fiddled with the controls again. "There you are. Now look."

First there was nothing but machines; some of them almost alien in conception, and then there was only one machine, something like a computer; but with a lot of ancillary equipment. After a while I realized that I was looking at a production line. Various odds and ends ran along the belt system, into and out of the machinery, emerging with some modifications each time.

It was, I decided, producing some very strange things indeed. Tetchum presided over the computer, occasionally pressing a button, or consulting a dial, and feeding in information through a keyboard. There was a fanatical gleam in his eyes while the peculiar end products rolled, ran, wheeled, and even walked off. A great spidery-legged thing with a number of long, slender rods moving around a huge, pineapple-shaped head like revolving antennae, sprang off the end of the belt, poised itself with evident purpose, and then strode out of the picture.

My friends, you can show me anything you like and, even though I have never set eyes on it before, I'll tell you its purpose. It's a gift I have. It goes with my ability to think in terms of continuous circuitry. Given one end of a circuit the rest falls into place immediately. As I say, it's a gift. You either have it, or you don't. So, when I saw this monstrous, metallic spider walking off into nowhere through the side of the picture area I knew, with reasonable certainty, what it was. It was designed to operate on the rough, terrible terrain of some place like the Moon, and it was a hunter. Anyway, I had seen the protruding snout of the weapon it carried in its head. It was designed to kill.

I straightened up and looked at Tetchum. "You should be drummed out of the human race," I told him. "You put machines before man. You know what I think?"

"Now wait a minute," he interrupted. "That was really a super-condensed version of all the passions and enthusiasms; the quintessential me. The id. As it happens," he added, with some dignity, "I have *my* id under complete control."

"Perhaps," I said. "But that doesn't alter the fact that that thing with the legs was a killer, wasn't it? And so were the others. The main producer was nothing less than a machine designed to invent other machines, and you were feeding it information about your own species. I saw you. That spider thing puzzles me a bit, though. It was designed for rough terrain, like the Moon, maybe. Why the Moon? There are only a handful of men there in the half dozen observation stations."

"It wasn't designed for the Moon. It was designed for some p.d.q. legging over masses of bomb rubble."

"Nice man! You really meant it, didn't you? What you had in mind was nothing less than total destruction of the human race."

He nodded cheerfully. "That's about the size of it," he admitted.

"Why?"

"Why was Benson smashing up the Elgin Marbles? You can't blame me for what a stranger does, and the id is a stranger to most of us, which is just as well. The nearer the id and the upper man get to each other the more calamitous it is likely to be for mankind. Take Hitler, for instance. . . ."

"We'll take you," I broke in. "I'm not at all sure that you are not a bigger menace. This thing could work. I know a logical producing agent when I see one. And that had all the hallmarks of a real process. Those killers were real. Isn't the cobalt bomb enough?"

"Quite enough." There was a hint of amusement in his voice, and it had begun to rile me. "But aren't you taking this too seriously? After all, it's just a fantasy. Although, well, I suppose if a machine of that kind was fed the necessary information it would come up with certain answers, which could be fed back until it had collated all the facts necessary to produce anything you wanted. Of course, you'd have to have a pretty good idea of what you were after to keep the programming down to reasonable proportions. You know, I think it was this machine that caught Benson's interest."

"I'm sure it was," I agreed. "Come on, let's tip it over the Level."

He spread himself across the machine. "What's the human race ever done for you that you are so concerned. Don't forget Benson is a member."

"That's a point," I admitted. "We'll mulct him first, and then we'll tip it over the Level."

"Over my dead body," he pronounced melodramatically.

"An added inducement," I snarled; "but I don't think the authorities would understand."

For want of a better plan I went and videoed Benson. I got his secretary first. She was an attractive honey blonde with a rather husky voice, and a fetching smile.

"Can I help you?" she asked.

"In a thousand ways, baby," I said appreciatively; "but I have to speak with your boss first."

"You'd like to speak to Mr. Benson?"

"I'm just about to close a deal with him for about a million credits," I told her; "but I'd rather talk to you. Are you doing anything tonight, sweetheart?"

"Yes," she said sweetly. "I'll be over at the Salvation

Hostel serving soup to the big-dealers. Would you like me to put your name down for a pair of shoes?"

"Would you like me to put your name down for two mink coats," I riposted gently. "Baby, you'll never be cold again."

"You say the nicest things," she said dreamily. "The nearest I ever got to mink was phantom fox."

"Dry your pretty eyes," I told her. "You've just struck oil. Do you think pea-sized diamonds are vulgar?"

"Not if they come by the dozen," she smiled. "I'll put you through to Mr. Benson."

"Did I get that date?" I asked.

"Of course. I'll keep the soup warm, lover boy."

"Good girl," I grinned. "I'll be the one with the expensive cigar, and the gold lamé suit."

The smile vanished. "Like a million unicorns," she said tiredly. "I'll put you through."

I don't think I have the right kind of face, somehow. I do better when I breathe on the scanning lens.

Benson glared at me as though I had just tripped him up. "Yes?" he rapped, frowning.

"How would you like to buy a sledge-hammer?" I inquired. "You could maybe smash up the Elgin Marbles."

He almost gasped. "How the hell did you get to know that? I told Tetchum to destroy the tape."

"He did," I said; "but you forgot about his memory."

"You've got the id-scope, then?" he said with commendable composure.

I smiled at him. "It's yours for a million credits."

His composure broke. I thought he was going to have a stroke. He fumed and snorted, and made a desperate effort to get his words out, and his face assumed the appearance of an almost perfectly round, red Dutch cheese. Finally, he managed it.

"I'll have the police on you," he blustered. "The id-scope

is my property. You stole it. It was legally mine, and you can't prove otherwise."

"Whatever the legality," I told him, "it's going to cost you a million to get your hooks on this invention."

He mopped his brow with a handkerchief drawn from his sleeve, and calmed down a bit. "You don't seem to have much respect for the rights of property," he remarked with a conscious effort.

"Correction," I said. "I haven't any. It's stacked the wrong way."

"I'll have to think about this," he said. "Where can I reach you?"

"You could try the Marleton," I told him. The Marleton is about the most expensive hotel in the city. "You won't find me there; but you could have a nice little chat with the desk clerk. He flips in the presence of his betters. Tell you what, I'll video you every hour on the hour for the next three hours. Not from the same call box in case you think of informing the police."

I switched off. We had him on toast. Or so I thought; but I should have realized that a man of Benson's experience would be no pushover. When I got back to the hideout Tetchum was being interviewed by a heavy-jowled police officer.

"This man will vouch for me," he said desperately when he saw me. "We've taken the place on a short lease."

"I never saw him in my life before," I declared. "I'm the sanitary inspector for the district," I added, and made for the door; but another cop, concealed behind this, grabbed me, and I found myself suddenly wearing a pair of handcuffs.

"You'll regret this," I warned him. "My father is mayor of the city, and I am related to your Chief by marriage."

"That should make the headlines," he grinned, "seeing

that the mayor is a bachelor. I wouldn't bank on the Chief, either. He's been known to work out on his in-laws."

Politics always bug me, somehow. "It must have been some other city," I said, "and some other time. Maybe ten years ago."

"Maybe some other country," he returned. "Maybe during the French Revolution."

I shrugged my shoulders. "All right," I sighed. "What's the charge?"

Still grinning, he turned to his colleague. "What was the charge, now? It sort of slipped my memory."

The other stared at me. "About everything except murder," he said morosely; "but we're working on that."

Just then Benson came hurrying in. "Ah, there you are, you damned, thieving scoundrels," he said unpleasantly. "We thought your hideout would be somewhere near the video box."

"It didn't take much figuring out after that," the morose one commented. "It had to be this place, and that's breaking and entering. There's also stealing an insured package while in transit. . . ."

"And extortion," Benson reminded him. He pointed at me. "This is the man who actually made the demand. He wanted a million credits."

The other police officer whistled. "Whee-ew! That's real big. A million credits, eh? Well, that's real big." He seemed happy.

"There seems to have been a misunderstanding," Tetchum said quickly. "This is not Mr. Benson's property. It's mine."

"It was under a distraint order," Benson said. "This man was an illegal sub-tenant in property leased to his late Aunt Agatha. One of the conditions of that lease was that there must be no sub-letting. . . ."

"Look," said the cop who had grabbed me, and who had now begun to look slightly harrassed, "let's keep this simple, huh? I'm no great shakes at unravelling leasehold tie-ups. So, if you don't mind, we'll start where Mr. Benson was shipping this thing from an address on Third Level to his own premises when it was presumably hoisted by two characters whom the evidence would suggest were these two." He nodded us into the deal. "Any objections to that?"

"Yes," I said. "I was doing the shipping, not Benson."

"That's right," agreed Benson; "but he had charged it up to me."

"That doesn't make it your property," the morose cop pointed out.

"As it stands it's useless to him, anyway," I said, smiling. "He could maybe copy it and make a few thousand quick credits; but the inner secret would be lost to him forever without the aid of the inventor, and of myself, of course. I think Mr. Tetchum will agree with me that this instrument is beyond price. It holds the key to immense power, and riches beyond calculation." I was watching Benson's face as I spoke, and I could see that he was rising to the bait. His Achilles heel was an over-developed acquisitiveness. When it came to cupidity he was wide open to the hook. "Yes, properly exploited," I went on, "this invention would enable an astute businessman to take over the entire wealth of the country and, given sufficient time, most of the universe as well."

"Nonsense," he said, and with the next breath: "Do you really think so?"

"Give or take a galaxy," I assured him. "But you need the right kind of technical know-how. You could hardly do better in this connection than engage the services of Tetchum, who is the actual inventor of this marvellous what-not, and in myself you have the greatest cyberneticist the world has ever known. I am a modest man, but I doubt if so much genius has ever been gathered together in one spot. You, too, Mr. Benson, have a not inconsiderable talent. . . ."

"What is this, Joe?" asked the cop who had handcuffed me. "Some kind of con trick?"

"I don't know," the other said slowly. "Let's run 'em in."

"Hold on!" said Benson agitatedly. "There may have been a misunderstanding."

"Quite so," I hastened to agree. "When I videoed your office I wasn't trying to take you for a million credits. I was merely trying to impress upon you that that's what you'd have to sink into the project before you could expect any real return. Afterwards it would be like a dam bursting. There aren't enough banks built to hold the kind of money this baby can make for you. Is it a deal?"

"Is what a deal?" he asked, suddenly cautious. "What do you get out of it?"

"If there's going to be that much money," argued Tetchum, "we don't have to quarrel how much each of us gets out of it. I just want a legal contract guaranteeing me a certain minimum percentage, and I want a lump sum now."

"Like a million credits," I said quickly.

"That's out of the question," Benson snorted. "Quite out of the question. We must go further into this. We'll adjourn to my office, and we'll have the id-scope taken there, too. I'll arrange that right away."

"When you've quite finished your Board meeting," the morose cop said wearily, "maybe we could get something else settled. Do you or don't you want us to arrest these men on any or all of the charges you were prepared to prefer against them about ten minutes ago. What about the breaking and entering?"

"I happen to own this building," Benson frowned, "and I should have thought by now that you would have seen that it was all, as I said before, a misunderstanding. I'm not preferring any charges, of course. Now, if you don't mind, kindly release this man. We have some important business to discuss."

The one who had put the handcuffs on me took them off again. "Hell!" he said. "Who'd be a cop?"

They went out. As they reached the door the morose one, whose name was Joe, turned and looked at me. "What's your name, mister?" he asked.

"Belov," I said. "Hek Belov."

"Yeah," he murmured thoughtfully. "That rings a bell. If you're not on the files I'm a monkey's uncle."

"Give my regards to your nephew," I said sweetly. "He's as cute as a cartload of cops."

He looked at me, bleakly. "Just don't get in my way again, mister," he said, "or I'm liable to remember that remark." He went out, and didn't close the door.

Benson videoed for a truck, and after the id-scope had been loaded on we climbed into his private hoverjet and went on ahead to his office.

We had to pass the blonde secretary, and I nodded to her. "What goes with mink, baby?" I asked.

Her eyebrows went up slightly; but she quickly recovered from the initial surprise at seeing me there. "I do," she said huskily. "But what happened to your white beard, and your long, red cloak?"

I grinned at her. "You must have missed *The Son of Santa* on the old slot haul. There's a repeat tonight, sweetheart. Bang a coin in at eight sharp. It'll sleigh you."

"Come on!" bawled Benson. "Time's money, and I pay for the time around here."

"I operate in and out of season," I added, before I followed Benson into his office. "Just let me know where you hang your stockings, honey."

"Flapdoodle," she said in a tired voice, and went on typing.

We set the id-scope up in Benson's sparsely-furnished office, and Tetchum adjusted it. Benson walked about like a caged animal. "That invention production line is what I want to talk about," he said, rubbing his pudgy hands together.

"It's running now," Tetchum told him. "Do you want to see it?"

"I've seen it, haven't I? What I want to know now is what the chances are of developing such a thing."

Tetchum shrugged his shoulders and looked at me. "The chances are excellent," I assured him quickly, although I held the contrary view.

One has to live.

He peered at me out of his little, red-rimmed eyes. "And how do you propose to set about the project?" he inquired directly.

"Well," I said with an easy, ingratiating smile, "I could draft you the various circuits right now. Tetchum will take care of the purely mechanical end, and we should have the first model ready to run in about ten years' time. We won't quarrel about salaries. Three thousand a month will do, and expenses, of course. By the way, you'd better let me have a blank cheque or two. There's the material to order. . . ."

"You're a crook!" Benson exploded furiously. "I should have had you jailed when I had the chance. Now, you listen to me, Belov. This machine has to be in basic production order within six weeks. You can take your time improving on it; but I must see that it is capable of devising and producing elementary items before I sink any real money into it. During this initial period I am willing to pay you a small wage, and you will be entitled to meal chits, which are exchangeable in our staff canteen.

"The same goes for Mr. Tetchum, except that I am willing to advance him the sum of three hundred credits as earnest of my intentions, and to seal any breach between us. Whatever materials you want can be ordered through my secretary. They will be approved only if I think them essential to the project. I have one simple, golden rule, and that is to keep expenses down. I am a successful business man because I know how to do just this. In any case, free capital is always difficult to arrange now that the Government is engaged in its new economy drive. To put it in a nutshell, so that you will know where you stand, I have very little money to invest in schemes of this nature; but I will do what I can."

All he had was a few odd millions or so, the cheese-paring old skinflint. "God bless you, Mr. Copperfield!" I said feelingly.

However, in these hard times a job's a job. It took about seven weeks to mock up the first version of Tetchum's auto-ventor, as he insisted on calling it; but, to tell the truth, I didn't really know what we'd got. The circuits I managed to dream up were logical within themselves, and applied to the necessary mechanical stages of the line, as we saw it in the id-scope, they fitted. Yet, taken as a whole it was a strange hotch-potch of unrelated units, and that had me puzzled.

We pronounced it finished largely because I had come to the end of the circuit sequence, and then Tetchum suddenly threw his hand in and accused me of fabricating circuits without regard to the ultimate project. I said I was trying to accommodate his meaningless mechanism. He said: "The hell! It's not going to work, anyway."

It didn't, of course. I gave it a last look over and almost groaned. It seemed a mass of odds and ends with whole sections that didn't do anything at all. I wiped my hands on a piece of rag and pointed to a mess of gears and levers perched like a mechanical praying mantis on top of what might easily have passed for an ancient clothes wringer. I didn't recollect seeing it in the id-sequence; but then not much of it did look like the original.

"What's that?" I asked, pointing.

"How the hell do I know?" he said petulantly. "I was trying to guess what some bit of your fatuous circuit was for, and that's how it came out. The way things are going we'll both land up in jail for fraud or something."

"It was your brainchild," I pointed out. "I don't see where I come into it. If a fraud has been perpetrated then, naturally, you are entirely responsible."

He gave a hollow laugh. "*My* brainchild?" he said. "That thing? That mechanical nightmare? It came from your twisted brain, that's what. I wash my hands of it."

"As a gentleman," I said with quiet dignity, "I can only treat such vulgar disparagement with the contempt it deserves—you gimmick-headed apology for a beetle-brained moron! Now listen to me, we've got to get this scrap-heap working somehow even if it's just long enough to convince old Benson that we have the right idea. Come on, man, buck up. We'll give the thing a trial run."

I switched the computer in, and gave the line start lever a half turn. As the power came in I brought it hard over. There was a roar from the aggrieved motors, and the mantis thing went mad. It flung itself round and round at a tremendous lick, and then shot off at an angle that just missed decapitating the luckless inventor. He screamed, and threw himself to the floor.

I switched off and helped him to his feet. "Supposing I'd been killed!" He sounded horrified.

"I'd have missed you," I assured him savagely, "like a hole in the head."

"Well, that wraps it up, anyway," he said. "That does it. I quit. I always knew I wouldn't get away with it."

"What do you mean get away with it?" I asked, as

a shrewd suspicion began to form in my mind. "This isn't . . . ? I mean you didn't . . . ?"

He nodded. "You might as well know the truth. It's all a lot of hokum. Id-scope and the lot. I faked it up from some pre-recorded film."

"But I saw myself with those delightful . . . I mean those disgusting females. I saw myself gorging like a famished swine. . . ."

"Yes, yes, I know. That was the only clever part of it. The features were blanked out in the original tape. It took me ages to get this right. I had to arrange for the viewer's face to be keyed into the space on the video tape. There's a hidden scanner that takes the necessary shots, adjusting the magnification as required, and the keying in is done from this. Of course the expressions aren't always right; but I was careful to ensure that the full face didn't appear too often. I'm out a few credits on the tapes; but it can't be helped. I've had enough of it. I'm turning it in right now."

"No you don't," I said, detaining him by the arm. "We're in this together. Besides, you just can't walk out like that. Benson would still be gunning for you. No, my poor friend, our only chance is to complete this ridiculous auto-ventor to specification. To Belov's specification. That is to say, it should be made to appear to work. Benson's greed will do the rest."

I nodded towards the extraordinary contraption that now almost filled the whole of the spare room that Benson had given us. "Watch it doesn't get away," I said. "I'm going for some lunch. I can't think on an empty stomach. My brain must be down there somewhere."

"I'll have a sandwich in the canteen," he said dejectedly.

"See you later," I said, "and give my love to the fat brunette with the skinny legs. She has a generous hand with the buttered toast."

I strolled into the rather broken down restaurant of my friend Emilio Batti. I found him operating with a carving knife on a huge ham. "Ah, Belov!" he greeted me affably. "I 'ave a nice roast beef today, or maybe you would like a porterhouse steak with all the trimmings, huh?"

"With all the trimmings," I nodded. "Lay it on, Emilio, and don't forget the cherry pie."

He beamed at me from under his tall, chef's hat; a *cordon bleu* in a slum restaurant. The great Emilio wasn't just a chef, he was an artist where food was concerned. His culinary creations could delight the heart of the gourmet or, for the same price, fill the gourmand up to his pig ears. Emilio was happy to cater for both.

"You 'ave money, of course?" he said, and his white, chef's hat seemed to take on an air of affability, too. Still smiling, he said: "I think maybe you have forgotten you still owe me thirty credits."

"I'll find myself a table," I said, non-committedly, and moved off.

"Belov!"

The windows rattled and the regulars covered their soup with napkins as the dust descended from the old ceiling. I came to a dead stop.

"Come back here, Belov!" thundered Emilio. "You 'ave no answer my question. Why won't you not answer, huh?"

I went back, and he waited for me; two-forty pounds on the hoof, and still clutching that enormous carving knife.

"I know you, Belov," he said. "Yesterday you 'ave money. Tomorrow you 'ave money. But today. . . ."

I spread my arms, and broadened the smile. "Today I have no money. A temporary embarrassment, old friend, I assure you."

"No, no, no!" he bellowed, thumping with one huge fist on the metal-topped counter. A heap of cheese sandwiches tilted and then fell towards me. I let them fall. If there's one thing I don't like above all other things in the food line it is cheese sandwiches. All the affability had gone now. Even his chef's hat had altered in shape and, moving forward, seemed to glare at me balefully.

He stuck the great, broad-bladed knife into the ham and leant across the counter, breathing garlic all over me. When he spoke again he was almost hoarse with suppressed rage.

"Belov, you 'ave not pay anything off the money you owe me. 'Ow you expect I pay my bills, huh? You think perhaps I should starve to death so that you can live and grow fat?" He removed the knife from the ham like Excalibur from the stone, and brandished it. "I should cut you off from your windpipe," he told me, and I drew back to a discreet distance. "Out of everyone else I make maybe a little profit; but you, Belov, are a stone around my old age savings. I think maybe before I am retiring I will be living off my own trash bin."

"All right, all right!" I snarled, seeing that there was nothing doing. "If that's the way you feel about it, you great, fat food spoiler, I'll take my custom elsewhere."

To my surprise he began to laugh. He laughed till the tears ran down his cheeks, and one customer, glancing round nervously, left in a hurry.

"I can wait," I said icily.

I waited until he began to dab his eyes with a kitchen cloth, the fit having subsided. "Well?" I asked. "What's so delirious about a hungry man?"

He shook his head and grinned at me. "'Ave a cheese sandwich," he invited, offering me one of those that remained on the plate.

I looked at them with disgust. "May lightning strike me if I do," I said, "you mountainous slob! I wouldn't insult my stomach by eating in your filthy restaurant. I only came here for a rest." I raised my voice for the benefit of the other customers. "This whole place is infested by rats and other vermin. One of these days the bubonic plague is going to slip out of your stinking kitchen and strike the city dead. Wild horses wouldn't get me in here again. I can tell you this. . . ."

"You are going to eat somewhere else, huh?" he said, still grinning. "Well, just this one time I chalk it up for you. I think maybe I should 'ave my 'ead examine, though. Rosie!" he shouted. "One porterhouse, and all on, for Mr. Belov."

"Don't forget the cherry pie," I reminded him, "and dowse it with fresh cream."

"What 'appen to the bubonic plague?" he sneered. "All of a sudden you like to eat 'ere, huh?"

"All of a sudden I am a liar," I told him.

When I got back old Benson was there. He was talking to Tetchum who looked distinctly uneasy. Benson looked like a fat, grotesque spider about to pounce on some luckless creature. He was walking up and down in front of the auto-ventor, and now and then he let his head turn slightly as he took another glance at our masterpiece.

"Well," he exclaimed, when he saw me, "if it isn't the great cyberneticist himself. I thought you'd have at least had the sense to flee the country." He regarded me with a crooked smile.

Mentally I cursed Tetchum, thinking he must have spilt the beans; but I played it cautiously, which was as well.

"I take it," I said, with heavy dignity, "that this is one of your funny jokes; but I'm afraid the point escapes me."

He swept a contemptuous arm towards the auto-ventor. "And this?" he inquired scornfully. "Is this one of *your* funny jokes?"

"That," I said, frowning, "is the auto-ventor. It may look a little rough; but we have certain modifications in hand with the object of streamlining the whole project. You won't know it in a week's time."

He glared at Tetchum. "You never mentioned anything about this," he said.

Tetchum looked uncomfortable. "It was to be a kind of surprise," he said weakly.

Benson's jaw jutted out. "Well, this won't be a surprise," he told us nastily. "If that thing isn't in production by tomorrow I'm going to call in the fraud squad. That's all. Tomorrow you deliver—or else. I believe in giving every man the benefit of the doubt."

When he'd gone Tetchum turned a gaunt, tired face to me. "I don't know how much of this I can stand," he said. "He'd been grilling me for nearly an hour when you came in. I almost broke down and confessed."

"Never do that," I advised him. "If he calls the police in hold out until the third rib goes. They've been known to have a change of heart."

"Like hell!" he said gloomily.

"Like apologizing and kicking you in the teeth," I agreed.

We went to work on the auto-ventor, trimming it down to a workable whole. The odd thing was that I had an inner conviction that it would run. What exactly it would produce was quite another matter. Mind you, a lot of these production units are pretty standard these days. As I saw it, you programmed the computer, outlining your approximate requirements, and these were interpreted and converted into impulses that controlled both the feed-boxes, with their component parts, or raw materials, and everything else as well.

The only trouble was that full programming was impossible without having previously invented the desired article. So, how do you programme a computer when you haven't a clue as to what you want, why you want it, or how it might be manufactured? Of course, the problem was much simpler than that, as I explained to Tetchum. All we had to do was make it appear to work.

"In other words you are compounding the original fraud. I don't think we should get in as deep as that."

Friends, I have never been so insulted in my life! That anyone should think that I, Belov, would lend himself to anything even remotely dishonest. I was mad, I can tell you.

"How dare you!" I said. "Do you think that I have so little respect for the integrity of my profession as to allow my name to be associated with a shake-down? I would never dream of defrauding a client. Look at it this way. Benson is prepared to pay good money—not much money, maybe, but good money—for what amounts to a virtual impossibility. Well, people do that every day. They pay to see a magician make someone, or something, vanish before their goggling eyes, or produce real rabbits from a phoney hat.

"It's all fake, of course; but that's what they pay for, and that's what they get. Does anyone ever accuse the magician of fraud? Of course not. A little legerdemain never hurt anyone. There it is, then. Benson is going to get some rabbits from an electronic hat or, if you like, a few goofy gimmicks from a fake production belt. What's the difference? Anyway, the kind of money he's prepared to lay out only entitles him to a seat in the stalls. He can't dictate the acts. That's our end."

In all truth, friends, he hadn't spent much. All we had was second-hand gear. Part of the production unit had been originally equipped for producing pocket videos, and the rest had been turning out and bottling a certain patent medicine before Benson acquired it. I don't know what he thought we might do with the weird and wonderful assortment of rubbish he dumped on us; but it was patent that he combined an immense moronic grasp of practical automated engineering with a touching, and childlike faith in the ability of the practical man to modify, make-do, and mend. Or maybe it was just that he was a mean, cheese-paring, gradgrinding, penny-shaving old knuckle-head.

After a deal of trial and error testing we finally had the thing produce something. I took the article off the end of the line and looked at it. As might be expected, the influence of the oddly assorted and now combined production units was very much in evidence.

Tetchum put it very succinctly, I thought. "It's a damned video in a goddamned bottle!" he said disgustedly.

"What did you expect?" I asked him. "The Russian Crown Jewels in an Egyptian sarcophagus?"

"A video in a bottle, eh?" he said, waxing sarcastic. "I reckon that beats ships four ways. Can't you just see Benson's face when we show him? Look, Mr. Benson, a video in a bottle? Don't that beat all?"

"It's the memory banks," I said. "They're soaked with the old processes. We'll have to replace them. I'll let Benson know the sad news. He'll have to spend more money. That should make him sick."

Benson, for once, took it quite calmly, apparently accepting my explanation, and the new memory banks were quickly installed. I was ready to re-programme a couple of hours later. First of all, however, I made some circuit alterations, and once I had started this inspiration took over. The circuits I saw stemming naturally from the initial alterations (made to eliminate any natural bias towards the old processes) were completely new to me. I re-bridged, plugged, and wired; but without any real idea of the overall effect.

In the circumstances I didn't see that it mattered very much. The computer, a Walls Vertical 13/13, compared the programmed information I fed in with the rest of the tape, and then indicated that new materials would be required. These were obtained, and I adjusted the control speed to Slow-Run. This would give the all-purpose multipoint shapers a chance to correct any inadequacies due to under-programming. Then I switched on.

When the first item was through I switched off again. I examined the object curiously. It was globular, and roughly a foot in diameter. The exterior was black plastic, and there were three metal studs or push-switches bunched together in one place. The whole thing weighed perhaps a pound.

"Well, that's it," I said, trying to sound enthusiastic.

Tetchum frowned at it, and then took it off me. "Yeah," he acknowledged; "but what does it do?"

It didn't seem to do anything. I tried to recollect what I'd programmed for. It seemed to me that I'd had something simple in mind that would provide an adult with a certain amount of amusement, happiness maybe; in fact an adult toy, perhaps what a practising nutcracker would refer to as a Queeg onanism-surrogate, God bless him! Something, in fact, that would be an improvement on two large ball bearings. I had included something about youthfulness being part of it, and fed in some information about the qualities of this true state of man.

The 13/13, incidentally, could be modified for purely intellectual tasks. The modification block, which was really a homeostatic-and-relative-reasoning-instrument, could be plugged in below the main chassis. I had a look. It was there all right.

"We've got an intelligent monster on our hands," I said. "This thing's got a decision box."

"Is that bad?" he asked.

That depended. It could reason to some extent; but, as with the human animal, this did not necessarily mean that it would take the right decisions. It might even make some very foolish mistakes. All that could be said for the set-up was that it was unpredictable. This particular unit was, in fact, still more or less in the experimental stage.

"Let's see what this globular gimmick does, and then we can either encourage it or whip the block out." I patted the computer affectionately on its casing. "You sly devil!" I said.

"I'll press one of these buttons and see what happens," Tetchum decided. "It doesn't seem to do anything," he frowned, with his head on one side listening, "except make a kind of humming noise." He wasn't standing where I was. I gazed at him in astonishment. "It's pleasant to handle, though. There's a sort of tingling that goes right through your body. Maybe that's what it does. It makes you feel good. I wonder if Benson would go for it?"

"In a big way," I assured him, as I found the use of my vocal chords again. I should say so. In fact, I was prepared to go bail that we had hit the biggest ever jackpot.

"I'll try the other buttons," he said cheerfully.

"Not yet." I backed off a bit. "Just press the same one again to see if it switches off."

"Okay." He pressed it while I watched with slightly bulging eyes.

There was a faint click, and he was his normal self again; a man who didn't even know that anything had happened to him.

"How do you feel?" I asked him, curiously.

"All right, I suppose; but I felt a lot better with the globe switched on."

"I expect you did. Well, as it appears to be quite safe you can hand it over and I'll show you what it does."

He handed it to me. "I know what it does. It just . . . Christopher! You look younger. About twenty years younger."

I took my finger off the button, and held the globe in

both hands, feeling good, feeling the new vitality coursing through my veins like cool fire.

"You look about eighteen," he said. "Is that how I looked?"

"Not quite so handsome," I said; "but, generally speaking, yes."

"Handsome nothing," he jeered. "It's just that you've lost all that ugly fat, and your face looks almost human." He looked down. "It hasn't done much for your feet, though. They're still as big as ever."

"All right, you can cut the pleasantries. I was being fitted for a brain when the good looks were handed out. A genius can't have everything. He should be thankful he hasn't got two heads. Anyway, we don't want to quarrel." I smiled. "We're in the big time. This is a rejuvenator; a gimmick with eternal youth on tap."

"Benson should be pleased," he said.

I glared at him. "Where does Benson come into it? I'm pleased. You're pleased. That's the full, limited company. Benson can go jump off the Level."

Tetchum looked worried. "Can we do that?" he asked anxiously. "After all, it's his money, and his premises. We happen to be employed by him, too; so the thing is legally, if not morally, his." He rubbed his hands together, and looked at me sidewise. "Do you think we'd get away with it?"

At this point Benson walked in and looked around. "Getting ahead with it?" he growled.

"As soon as we iron out the labour troubles," I told him.

"What the hell are you talking about," he demanded. "I never have any labour troubles. With the huge reservoir of unemployed that we have I am in a position to pick and choose. Anyone starts spouting and out he goes. There's a whole raft of men outside just waiting for his job. I never have labour troubles."

"You have now," I told him, imperturbably. "Serious labour troubles. In fact, the whole future of this important project is in jeopardy."

"All right," he gritted. "All right, then. Let's have it. What kind of labour troubles?"

"My colleague and I," I said, and Tetchum looked at me sharply, "require an immediate advance of salary—otherwise, to put it bluntly, the job stops."

Benson looked as though he would have liked to knock me down. He turned to Tetchum. "You're not in with him on this, are you?"

Tetchum shrugged his shoulders and looked uncomfortable.

Benson glanced from one to the other of us, and then he took a long look at the auto-ventor. Maybe the thought of all those possible millions escaping from his grasp was the deciding factor. "I can let you have a small advance," he told us, and got his cheque book out.

"Fifty credits each," I said, "made out to drawer."

"Make it a hundred," Tetchum said quickly, his cupidity having been aroused, I suppose, by the sight of the cheque book.

"I won't up the bidding," I smiled. "A hundred each will do nicely."

He gave me a single, venomous look, and then wrote in the amounts. "Here," he said, handing us the cheque. "This is the last, and you'd better get results soon." He smiled like a shark. "You've got about twelve hours, and then I intend to take certain steps, which may include seeking both technical and legal advice. I don't like being blackmailed, and I don't like being cheated."

After he'd gone I switched the line in, and we ran off thirty-six of the rejuvenators. These we stashed behind some empty plastic crates.

"Come on," I said to Tetchum. "We're going to celebrate. It's time we finished for the day in any case."

We cashed the cheques and I put some money in an envelope, addressing it to Emilio's Restaurant with a note which said, simply: *"All is forgiven. Belov."* I dropped it into a mail delivery chute, and stuck a dime in one of several adjacent slots for the stamp imprint. Then we went on the town.

Late that evening we returned to Benson's. We had some idea about removing the programming tape, and taking the rejuvenators. Our intentions after that were a bit vague; but we were both agreed that Benson just didn't figure. He'd got all the money he could usefully use. We needed all the money we could usefully acquire. We told the janitor that we had some important work to do, and he let us in.

We hadn't been there five minutes when, inevitably, Benson showed up. The janitor had probably videoed him. He came steaming in and swept over us. "As I thought," he said, when he'd had a good look round, and settled down. "You've been drinking." He poked a fat finger in my chest. "In my leisure moments, which are few, God knows, I study psychology. . . ."

"You surprise me," I said. "I always thought you had a headful of abacus beads."

"I study psychology," he went on, ignoring the interruption. "Now then, I believe there are three circles. The first and innermost circle, which is yourself, the next circle surrounding this, which is your relatives and immediate friends, and the great outer circle, which is the world at large. You, Belov, never go outside the first circle. You are, in fact, completely selfish. You should remember that man is not sufficient unto himself alone. He is not, if I may put it that way, an island."

This was probably the standard homily that he delivered to his erring employees. Coming from him it was a laugh.

"Very Frungian," I said, a bit thickly. "Man is not an island, eh? Well, I'm in agreement with you there. The infinitude of stars and planets, all and everything, galaxies and space-time continuums (did you know there was more than one, and one for every one of us?) jostle for recognition inside his tiny cranium. Man is not an island; but an entire universe, and there are as many universes as there are men."

"You're crazy!" Benson told me.

Tetchum looked at me gravely for a moment, swaying slightly, and then made a similar pronouncement.

"You're a nut!" he said.

I remembered what I'd heard about a treasured acting system called The Method, and concentrated on looking ovoid and hairy. It seemed important at the time. "I'm a coconut," I agreed. "In my belly swirls the Milky Way." I belched. "Hearken to the music of the spheres."

For a minute Benson looked as though he was about to explode, and then he gave way to an exasperated sigh. "Outside, both of you. I'll see you tomorrow when you're sober." He ushered us out, and left with just a parting curse. I got Tetchum to his lodgings on Third Level, and then went home myself.

The next morning I breakfasted off black coffee and lay down again. When I awoke it was getting on for eleven o'clock; but I felt less woolly. I got up, cleaned my teeth, endured a cold shower and, putting on some fresh clothes, I went out for breakfast. I arrived at Benson's just after he had returned from a quick, and probably indigestible, lunch. In fact, he followed me into the lift.

"Good morning," I said, putting a face on it.

"Good nothing!" he exploded. "Tetchum managed to get in early. What happened to you?"

"I couldn't get my head through the door," I told him,

"and I didn't like leaving it behind. I don't seem to think so well without it."

He glared at me; but forbore to reply, and I followed him out of the lift at the ninth floor. We walked in on Tetchum and found him sitting on a chair looking a bit pale around the gills.

"Never again!" he swore, when he saw me. "I think I've been poisoned. You're looking pretty good," he added enviously.

"That's because I know when to give in. What you could do with is a glass of cod liver oil with congealed cream. . . ."

He couldn't get out of the room quick enough.

"Well now, perhaps I could have a report on progress so far," said Benson. "If you don't mind," he added sarcastically.

"Not until my colleague gets back," I said. "It wouldn't be fair."

I lit a cigarette and sat down. Benson walked up and down like Felix, hands clasped behind him and head slumped in frowning thought. Once or twice he went over to the auto-ventor and looked at it. When Tetchum got back looking, if anything, paler, Benson nodded to him.

"Is this thing working?" he wanted to know.

"Yes," he said, just as I came in with a definite "No."

He gave us that old-fashioned look. "Yes or no?" he said. "Well, there's one way to find out."

Before I could do anything about it he had switched on, and the line began to roll. We stood there watching rather helplessly. When the black globular end product slid free Benson switched off again, and looked at me accusingly.

"I meant it wasn't working to our complete satisfaction," I told him, half apologetically.

"What does this thing do?" he asked Tetchum.

Tetchum looked at me, rubbed his hands together, and mumbled incoherently.

Our position had become untenable. The limited company of two had, it seemed, to be expanded to include the chief shareholder.

"You've another thirty-six of them behind those crates over there," he added, to our dismay. Poor Tetchum almost gibbered with embarrassment and the fear of Bensonic reprisals. "I get in early," he said, "and I have duplicate keys to every door in the building." A frosty smile spread over his fleshy features. "What were you trying to pull, Belov? It was your idea, wasn't it?"

I put on a hurt look. "I don't know what you have in mind," I protested; "but I assure you that everything is very much above board. Those globular items you saw behind the crates are rejects. The one you hold now may be the same. We'll have to test it, won't we." I made a quick decision. In or out? He was in. "Just press the top button," I directed. "You are due for a pleasant surprise."

He hesitated for a second and then pressed the button switch. Youth hit him suddenly. He staggered as his paunch vanished and his centre of gravity shifted.

"Do you always undress in public?" I asked him quietly.

"Eh?" he said, and looked down at himself. His pants were draped round his ankles, the waist that held them having contracted some eight or nine inches.

He put the globe down and pulled his pants up. He still didn't get it. "What the hell happened?" he asked. He sounded more annoyed than puzzled.

"Poltergeists," I told him. "It goes on all the time."

"Nonsense!" he snorted, and looked at the ball accusingly. "I got some kind of a shock from that piece of apparatus. It probably made my stomach muscles contract. Yes, that must be it. It's some kind of party gag, isn't it?"

"Could be that," I said; "but it does have another purpose. All right," I nodded to Tetchum. "Show the gentleman."

Tetchum took the globe in both hands. It was still switched on so the change was instant. Benson shook his head slowly from side to side, and a little wondering sigh escaped from his lips. "It can't be," he said. "How can it be? A rejuvenator. How can it possibly work?"

"Like everything else," I said, "the explanation is a fairly simple one. The wonder is in not knowing. Once it has been done people wonder why it wasn't done before."

I don't think he heard me. "This is really something," he enthused. "Yes, this is really something."

Tetchum switched off and was immediately his normal self.

Benson frowned. "What's this?" he demanded. "Is it an illusion or something? Isn't it permanent?"

"It depends what you mean by permanent," I told him.

He threw his arms about. "Now look here, you'll just have to improve on it, that's all. I'm not paying for half a job."

"Thanks for the encouragement," I said. "Your generous appreciation is almost overwhelming."

"Just a minute." Benson had a faraway look in his eyes, as though he had seen a vision of Fort Knox wide open and unguarded. "Now if you could scale this thing down to pocket size it would become a commercial proposition. Everyone would want one."

"Yes, sir, Mr. Benson," I said, throwing him a salute. "Scale it down to size. Miracles are ten-a-penny, and fashions change. What we want now are vest-pocket miracles. The sunset over ancient Petra perhaps in a pea-sized attachment for a key-ring; instant blondes in tablet form; Paradise in little boxes, and eternal youth in a simple pocket pack."

Benson wasn't listening. "We must keep costs down, of course. I think if we aimed at selling this product at, say, ten thousand credits with full credit facilities that should bring it within the reach of most people. After all, this is a democracy, and we should try and ensure that the greatest possible number benefit from the device."

"Even the unemployed shouldn't have much difficulty in raising the deposit," I said. "All they have to do is rob a bank."

Benson, still with that faraway look in his eyes, smiled almost happily. "Just carry on along the lines I have indicated," he told us. "I'm going to engage a patent attorney to nail down my rights in this invention."

"*His* rights!" exclaimed Tetchum, after Benson had left. "What damn nerve! Haven't we any rights? All he did was supply a litttle money."

"What does he ever do?" I asked. "Don't tell me you're looking for justice. That way madness lies."

"Never mind," sighed Tetchum; "but if we only knew how it worked we could maybe force him to share the patent rights. I should think knowing how it worked would be an important point in our favour." He looked at me. "Didn't you say you knew how the thing worked?"

I nodded. "It happens to fit in with my own theory of life and death. I could be wrong; but I don't think so. In a phrase it's what I should call image transference. All along the dotted line from the womb to the tomb man is subjected to a kind of quantum existence. He has no permanent fleshly home. His spirit, or the Life Force if you like, jumps from static body to static body, because there is no such thing as movement. Movement is only apparent, as it is in a film. The forms are fixed from beginning to end. They only appear to move.

"The Life Force moves through thousands of these 'film-fixed' image-forms in the course of a second and, of course, they get older and older and more decrepit as what we call Time goes on. Unless, maybe, there's a series just around the corner, all smashed up by a slew of similarly immobile trucks; an accident, you see, that has no meaning in Time until the Life Force touches it. The agony you suffer is the agony of the pulsating Life Force fiercely trying to carry on and through. . . ."

"What happened to free will?"

"That's another story," I said. "You've only heard the half of it."

He waved a careless hand. "Never mind. Just tell me how the rejuvenator fits into all this."

"I think it's time-tuned and when you press the right button, image transference takes place. What actually happens is that the younger images are being whipped out from a certain point in time that can be simply designated as a couple of decades ago, or thereabouts. The snag is that they are being replaced by your present image-forms. In other words you are laying a trail of grandfathers, which you will meet next time round; that is, if you believe in Nietzsche's theory of eternal recurrence. It could create a few problems to say the least of it. One day you're young and the next you're middle-aged, and then you're young again. They'd probably put you away." I held the globe and pretended to switch it on and off. "Now I'm old; now I'm young. What a parlour game!"

Tetchum's mind had wandered on to something else. "We'll be famous," he said, with a silly smile on his face. It seemed to please him.

"Like Jekyll and Hyde." Some of the possible consequences were becoming clearer to me. "Tcha! If we had any feeling for humanity we'd smash the whole stinking lot, and jam them down Benson's rapacious throat."

It was just a fake. A beautiful fake. The youthfulness only formed to what the chemist would call a clathrate compound. There would be a transfer of matter; but no actual marriage of mind and body. The two would be held together merely by some cross-dimensional equivalent of the feeble van der Waals forces.

"The other two buttons," said Tetchum suddenly. "What about them? What do they do?"

"Press them and see," I suggested, and offered him the plastic globe.

He took it and then somewhat hesitantly pressed the nearest button. I was astonished to see a strange, hairy face glaring at me with a mixture of fear and primitive hate. I stood my ground, of course; although just for that split second my legs seemed powerless to move me anyway.

The atavism, its nostrils dilating, took a quick, traumatic glance around the room, and dropping the globe, howled like a dog. The globe hit the floor and rolled away. The electronic spell was broken, and it was Tetchum before me again. He clapped a hand to his mouth, and stopped howling.

"Welcome home," I said with immense relief. "I just had an ancestor of yours here; but he didn't like the place. He'd never seen a cave like it."

"So that's what it does," said Tetchum. "Well, I'm not pressing the other damned button. You can do it yourself. Here." He picked up the black globe intending to pass it to me; but somehow or other he must inadvertently have pressed the remaining switch.

A heap of clothes dropped to the floor and, for an instant, that's all there was of Tetchum; but as the globe rolled clear the clothes leapt up again with their poor, bemused owner inside them.

"What happened?" he asked, a bit shakily. "That was dead rough."

"Well," I said, "I'd hazard that you died without issue. It was probably a slice of the future, and there just weren't any more Tetchums in your direct line."

"I'm not handling the blasted things at all after this," he

told me. "There's something screwy about the whole business. I watched you programme the computer, and on the basis of that all you should have got was some kind of super yo-yo. Even though it has that decision box I don't see how it could possibly produce anything of the order of this globe with the information in its memory banks. They were clean till we got hold of them. Those tools, too. . . ."

"I know," I said. "They just aren't up to the kind of work that must have gone into the globe, although you must remember that we don't know what's inside there yet."

I had given it some thought, though, and I could see that the position transducers, for example, carried by the circulating ball screws, were not really up to a precision job of the kind this must be.

"I'm not sure I'd want to dismantle one," said my colleague. "In fact I am sure that I won't. You can do it. I'll watch from a safe distance."

"Of course there's the Uncertainty Principle," I pointed out, as I thought aloud on the general question of how the production line had come up with such an extraordinary gimmick. "Heisenberg said that the operator is necessarily involved in any experiment, and fundamentally this *was* an experiment."

"Which operator? Not me, and not you; so what does that leave?"

"The computer? After all, it has a sort of extra brain."

Each of the globes was a single, plastic whole. I had to saw through one all the way round and separate the two halves in order to see what was inside.

There was nothing that I'd ever seen before. It took a while to register; but I decided it looked like a mass of tiny dots. They were shifting and reforming in each half of the globe, and now and then they changed colour. They were on the verge of an entirely new experience.

"That settles it," Tetchum said. "There isn't anything in the supply vats and magazines that could produce this weirdy."

I unclipped the service panel and took a look at the "decision box"; but it didn't help. So I switched the line in and watched it produce a couple of globes. The big question was what happened to the solid-state amplifiers that the programming had specified. They weren't in the globes. That was another thing. I had programmed for a square mould; but the machine had apparently had other ideas, and the plastic form-beds had been adjusted accordingly. The slides took the amplifiers into the mould and that meant that they should have been sealed in the globe, only they weren't.

Behind the plastic supply vat there was another inspection panel. I removed this and watched the black globes form. The solid-state amplifiers moved into this spot all right, and then what? I shut off the vat and saw, with amazement, that the amplifiers were going through the solid steel bed, and something else was popping up in their place.

Tetchum almost beat me to the door, where we stood half in and half out of the room looking at the balls of node points, or whatever they were, their full luminosity revealed, moving along the line without the plastic containers. As they reached the end of the operational belt they were rejected by the electronic eye of the sorting gate, which junked them into a box as below tolerance.

"Why didn't you switch off, you cowardly swine?" I asked Tetchum.

"What about you? I didn't see you wait around when you saw the amplifiers dropping through the bed."

"Do I have to do everything around here?" I asked him. "You were nearer to the switch."

"And you were nearer to the door. If I hadn't got over

here sharpish you'd have locked it behind you. I know your type. You want me to pull your chestnuts out of the fire. Well, it's no dice."

That's the way it goes, friends. You help a man out; but as soon as anything goes wrong it's no longer his problem—it's yours. Do a fellow a good turn and he won't rest until he sees you in jail. Tcha! Sometimes I despair of humanity.

I'd noticed a long tube of metal lying against the wall, and it struck me that this might provide the answer. If Tetchum was too craven to switch the thing off then I, Belov, would do it. I picked it up.

"What are you going to do with that?" he said.

The answer trembled on my lips; but I am, after all, a gentleman. I shouldered him out of the way.

"Move," I told him, "you chicken-hearted wretch! If I don't come back, lay a wreath on my statue. They're bound to erect one."

I advanced two paces; but was unable to reach the switch with the tubing. I took another step; but I was still about six inches short. I looked back at Tetchum. "Keep that door open," I said. "I might have to move rather fast."

"Oh, for heaven's sake!" he exclaimed, and walking past me he switched off.

I watched, fascinated; but nothing happened to him. Damned glory grabbers! The place is lousy with them. I threw the tubing down in disgust, and went over to the reject box to take a quick peek at the contents. It was empty. While I was standing there the last luminous node ball rolled down the reject trough, fell into the box, and burst like a brightly-coloured bubble.

Tetchum had a nasty smile on his face. "Well," he said, "haven't you got an explanation? Doesn't the great genius know just what is going on?"

I considered strangling him, and only the legal consequences of such an action deterred me. "As it happens," I rejoined with some heat, "I know precisely what's going on."

Actually, I had only some vague theories; but now, as happens sometimes, they began to fall into place, and I was convinced that I had the answer; something that covered all the facts and had its hooks in the unknown as well.

"Okay," said Tetchum annoyingly, "expound." He folded his arms, and waited.

"Very well," I agreed; "but I must warn you in advance that this is liable to tax your tiny brain beyond endurance. I'll keep the complications to a minimum, and just rough it in for you."

"You're just waffling. You don't know, do you?"

I went over to the machine and lifted an amplifier off the belt. "What's this?" I asked him.

"A simple K-type amplifier."

I shook my head. "As far as the machine, or I should say the computer, is concerned that's a key. A key to Chaos. My guess is that this is anything but a simple K-amp. The bit about youthfulness was the barb. I programmed that as part of an explanation; but the computer has referred to its standard banks, and got some other answers, which it chewed over in that decision box, the homeostatic part of the set-up. The result was that the computer was faced with something of an insoluble problem. It knew what to produce; but the materials weren't available, not all the materials, that is.

"Now this is where we have to make a leap in the dark. Here we are, a speck in the cosmic eye. The tiniest of tiny islands, where two and two make four, and logic—our peculiar brand of logic—holds sway. Outside, and everywhere, the primal stuff of the universe patterns itself crazily on stray thoughts escaping from the odd, alien, organism in its midst, because Chaos has its own logic. The logic of perfect illogicality. The infinite patterning that both is and isn't, now and forever, in the shifting never-never land of everything and everywhere and nothing anywhere. That's what lies outside the mind; but it doesn't lie outside the mental scope of a machine. A machine has no fear, and only the mental reservations with which man, in his wisdom, endows it. . . ."

"Cut the prologue and get to the explanations," said Tetchum impatiently. "I still think you're waffling."

"All right," I said, "if I have to come down to your moronic level this is the explanation. To get its raw materials our computer simply worked out that a certain electronic action would key out this primal material, and once it had passed the barrier it would accommodate itself to whatever logical process offered. In other words, the computer was able to key it out and shuffle it around to the desired artifactual lump of working matter. It's a kind of magic. The old workers of magic recognized no logical barriers either. Lay hands on the primal stuff and you can do anything with it. The difficulty is in breaking through the barrier. It happens the other way quite often. Apparitions are probably due to primal matter breaking through the barrier from the other side and forming themselves around stray thoughts. Where do you think ectoplasm comes from, and the echo of our own thoughts in strange, or remembered voices?"

"I won't argue with you," Tetchum said tiredly. "Maybe you do know. I don't suppose anyone else will ever know; but *you* know. Let's leave it there, All I want to know now is how we can collect from Benson, and then get the hell out of here, as fast as possible? I'm in favour of getting out anyway, money or no money. Something tells me we are approaching some kind of a crisis. My nerves won't stand much more of this."

"You're not even thinking straight. All we have to do is

wait for Benson to show up again, and turn the whole project over to him for a nice lump sum apiece."

"He won't let us go. You'll see." Tetchum sounded distressed. "What I need is a drink. Are you coming?"

"No, I'll hang on for Benson. You can bring something back."

He nodded and went out.

While I waited for Benson I tried the globes again. They seemed to be working okay, although I only tried the rejuvenation button. I wondered if the machine was still in order, and remembered that I'd turned the plastic supply vat off. I turned it on again, switched the line in, and walked away fast. Standing by the door I watched the plastic globes roll off the belt, and decided that everything was moving nicely again. I went back and switched off.

Everything would have remained that way, too, if I hadn't had time on my hands and an acute attack of curiosity. I felt I had to know just what happened to these chaos-keying electronic gadgets. There was no inspection panel under the plastic supply vat, because there was nothing under that part of the line anyway. One way to see what was going on was to remove part of the front slide process. This would leave a gap through which the point where the solid state devices were being squeezed could be observed.

I must have had a rush of courage to the head, otherwise I should never have attempted it. The slides were the quick release type, and easily removed. I could see right underneath now. At the moment there was no sign of anything out of the ordinary; but just wait till you switch the line in, Belov, I thought. My hand hovered over the switch for a few seconds in nervous indecision, like a fluttering bird chary about alighting; but I finally brought it down, and pegged the lever over, determinedly. Then I went and looked through the gap in the machine bed.

Removing that section of the line merely meant that the globes would not be equipped with switches. They rolled by just the same, and I bent down to peer underneath the matrix. I found myself watching the quondam amplifiers fall through the inch-thick steel bed, and into a thin, blue circle of light, a few inches below.

Rimmed by this phenomenon were things I couldn't begin to name, senseless patterns and frightening colours that mocked the spectrum; a whole boiling of things, swirling, patterning, and re-patterning. As each crystalline unit dropped into the circle of blue light a definite pattern, similar to a Maltese cross and grey in hue, flicked across the surface. Simultaneous with this a puff ball of tiny light points was flung upwards, through the steel and into the waiting globe.

I switched off quickly. Before the line had come to a stop I was on the other side of the door, turning a much more ordinary key. "I'm going for a drink," I croaked to the empty corridor, and staggered outside.

I got back at about three o'clock, and soon after Tetchum came in. He grinned at me, swaying as though he were in a high wind. "I feel much better now," he announced thickly. "Much, much better." He handed me a bottle of beer.

I looked at it, disgustedly. "If you'd stuck to that you'd have been all right, you miserable swine!" I told him.

He nodded, amiably. "Quite so. Quite so." For a while he watched me checking through the slides for the switch placement. Then he picked up the length of tubing I had left near the computer, and tried to twirl it in his fingers like a baton. "Too heavy," he said, picking it up off the floor and trying again. "Rah! Rah! Rah!"

I could see he was going to be a nuisance; but I had an

idea that I could sober him up in just about three seconds flat with a glimpse of that hell-hole under the machine bed. I switched on, and invited him to have a look. "Here's something," I said. "Just take a gander at it."

He bent over the gap and peered myopically at the blue ring and its associated phenomena. "Pretty," he said, appreciatively, and jabbed the metal tubing down into it before I could stop him.

There was a crash to the left of the computer, and I saw a foot-wide hunk of plascrete from the wall lying on the floor. A piece of tubing had come right through the wall, and was waggling about. I looked at Tetchum. He was happily stirring the contents of the blue-ringed hole. Some kind of cross-dimensional shift was displacing the tubing in real space.

"Stop that, you damned fool!" I shouted, and made a grab for the tubing. The next instant a section of it appeared in mid-air. I looked at it in stupefaction. "That was a big one!" breathed Tetchum, trying to jab something in the chaotic depths, and the piece of tubing I'd just caught sight of drove through the opposite wall at an acute downward angle.

There was the unmistakable sound of metal impinging on metal, and then a lighter thud. I pulled Tetchum away; but not before there were some other, odder sounds closer to hand, thunder in a minor key, with a sort of screeching accompaniment. I noticed then that the computer lights had gone out, and the line had stopped.

I left Tetchum, and had a look through the hole in the wall where the tubing had gone, to see what had happened on the other side, which was, in fact, Benson's private office, and holy of holies, where no one else was allowed; not even his secretary. I saw that the tubing had gone through the top of the safe which was parked hard against the wall at this point. It had apparently burst the door open. Some of the contents, papers mostly, lay scattered on the floor. The piece of tubing was imbedded in the grey carpet.

I found the rest of the tubing when I examined the computer. It was about six feet in length and it had gone right through the thing. "That's it," I announced. "You've speared its heart, liver, and lights. It's gone clean through the decision box. I think perhaps you'd better tell Benson the bad news. I may have to visit a sick aunt rather suddenly."

I was talking to myself. Tetchum had curled up on the floor, and had gone to sleep. He had the smile of an innocent little child; but he was snoring like a pig with its throat cut. I resisted the temptation to kick him, and dragged him into a corner out of the way, placing some empty crates about him. He'd stopped snoring, which was just as well, because Benson came in as I walked back to the computer. I wondered if he'd believe me if I swore we had been struck by lightning. I didn't think so, somehow.

He had a tall, gaunt-looking, middle-aged man with him. "Belov," said Benson, introducing us, "this is Mr. Swift. He's a patent attorney." He extended a soft, white flipper and we gripped, perfunctorily. "I had some difficulty in convincing him about the rejuvenation globes," Benson added. "Well, shall we have a demonstration?"

"I must confess," said the patent attorney, choosing his words with care, "that I am far from convinced in regards to this, er—somewhat extravagant claim. However, if you should care to demonstrate the, um—piece of equipment, no doubt I shall be able to form an, um—er, decision. I should perhaps warn you that I am not easily, hrrumph—deceived." He nodded to Benson. "Whenever you like my, er, um—dear sir."

I chose a globe at random, and handed it to Benson. "Perhaps you'd better try it yourself," I said, "or Mr. Swift may think I'm, um—dealing from the, hrrumph—bottom."

"That might be advisable, hrrumph," said the attorney; "but I shall need a great deal of, um—convincing just the same. I shouldn't like to, er, um—advise my client to spend, hrrumph. . . ."

"Yes, yes, Swift," said Benson impatiently. "We know you've got the best interests of your clients at heart, and you only cut yourself in on the profitable inventions. Now let's get on with it."

Swift frowned at him. "Very well," he agreed coldly.

"Watch," Benson told him. He pressed the middle button, and looked down towards his feet. He pressed again, and kept on pressing. Nothing happened. "Get me another globe," he grated.

He tried several while the puzzled patents attorney looked on. He turned to me. "What exactly, um, er—is supposed to happen?"

"He's waiting for his trousers to fall down," I said.

Benson glared at me; but went right on pressing and cursing, trying other globes, and then discarding them.

Mr. Swift looked from one to the other of us. "Why?" he asked, at last.

"That's the way youth hits him," I explained. "Nothing else changes. He was born with that face."

"Belov," said Benson in a tight voice. "I think you'd better start explaining. Why won't these things work? And where's that damned Tetchum?"

"He went out rather suddenly," I said, and went over to the bench to examine the globe we had sawn through. It seemed to me that the tubing, in piercing the computer's homeostatic brain, had wrecked the whole emprise. The stuff of Chaos had been drawn back again through that break in the barrier, or had just ceased to exist because of the change in the pattern of forces now that the computer's influence was broken.

One look at the two halves of the globe confirmed my worst suspicions. They were completely bare; the winking points of light had disappeared. I took another globe and, watched by both Benson and Swift, I cut through it while Benson swore softly to himself in a half-demented fashion. The attorney cracked his fingers nervously and hrrumphed until Benson told him to shut up.

This globe, too, was innocent of everything except the switching arrangement. I showed it to Benson.

"Where's the blasted amplifier?" he wanted to know. "I saw those things going through the line. Why isn't there one in there? Are they all like that? Now look here, Belov . . ."

"No, *you* look here," I interrupted. "They weren't amplifiers and nothing like them was ever in the globes. What was in the globes has gone down a kind of cross-dimensional drain."

"Oh, the hell with that for a tale!" he snorted. "Switch the line in and make some more."

It didn't seem a good time, somehow, to tell him that the line was *kaput*. That it would never produce anything of that nature again.

I waved my hand towards it. "You switch on," I said.

"You're finished!" he said in a choking voice. "Get off my premises before I call the police!" He pointed dramatically to the door. "Get out!"

"I want to see you switch on first," I said mildly.

He looked as though he would have liked to have taken me bodily and thrown me out into the corridor; but I smiled sweetly at him. "Watch out for the motor," I warned. "It's that stinking, old second-hand one you got from some junkyard. The commutator sticks."

"I'll deal with you later," he promised, and went over to the machine.

The attorney looked slightly petrified. "He's really quite

a nice fellow," I told him. "It's just that he has ingrowing toenails right the way through to his liver."

"Hrrumph," he commented, and cracked his fingers some more.

I watched with some interest while my erstwhile employer switched the line in.

The next instant found us all diving for cover as half-formed globes, bits of components, and even some of the slides shrapnelled about the room. I hid under the bench with the hrrumphing Swift, while Benson, who was lying out in the middle of no-man's land, glared balefully at us, and mouthed obscenities.

Right in the middle of it all Tetchum got up from behind the crates, and stormed at with shot and shell, as it were, staggered across the room until he reached Benson's recumbent form.

"You fat pig!" he said, with a catch in his voice. "Why won't you let us go?" Then he collapsed across the astonished tycoon.

Just then the machine stopped throwing things and ground to a halt. We came out from under the bench, and I hoisted Tetchum to his feet. Benson seemed to have had most of the wind knocked out of him; but he was trying desperately to say something.

"Good-bye," I said to him. "We'll send the bill for our out-of-pocket expenses, such as the fare for the helicab we're going to get now, by the third of next month. That'll give you time to hock your cuff links."

Swift bent down to help the purple-faced Benson, who had got to his knees. He brushed him off roughly. "Let go of me, goddamn you!" he wheezed.

I half-dragged, half-carried Tetchum down the corridor and into the outer office. Benson's honey-blonde secretary looked faintly surprised. "What happened to him?" she asked.

"He had an accident," I told her. "He was going for a glass of milk when he tripped over a brewery. By the way, baby, you'd better inform brother Benson that his safe's bust wide open. That was another accident."

She jumped to her feet immediately and ran off. I gazed after her hurrying form with some astonishment; but not without appreciation for those beautiful callipygian movements that one always associates with the female of the species. "What wicked thoughts are these that assail you, Belov?" I said. "A man of your age. Tch! Tch!"

Tetchum turned his glazed eyes upon me. "The hell with you!" he mumbled, and tried to drag himself away.

I got him to the lift and went down through all the Levels. We came out in the block shopping centre, where someone had thoughtfully provided an ice-water dispenser. I balanced Tetchum against the wall; but he slid slowly down to the polished floor.

I took two cartons of ice-water and bunged them against his hot, little ears. His eyes almost shot out of his head. He stood up, a bit unsteadily; but he stood up.

"I'll kill you!" he said, and fell against me.

I got one arm around his neck, and we went stumbling out into Low Level with Tetchum making blind swipes at me with his free arm. "I'll slaughter you!" he said.

I trundled him into a little eatery, and ordered coffee. "White for me," I told the girl there, "and black for my friend, with just a spot of salt."

"I'll kill him!" Tetchum told the girl brokenly. "I'll tear his head off!"

"Not in here," she said imperturbably. "It's my turn to clean the place out."

When she came back with the coffee she said: "They just flashed your picture on the video. What'd you do? Rob a bank?" She seemed delighted. "I never met a wanted man before. The boss is getting on to the police. He said that's what you are, a bank-robber."

"That was yesterday," I said; "but you know how they are in this city. Anyone would think I made a habit of it." I slapped a note on the counter. "Fill him up with coffee till his eyeballs turn brown, and then throw him out. I must leave at once. I've a very urgent appointment in South-East Peru, or somewhere even further in the opposite direction."

I was three Levels up and halfway across town when the riot can screamed down and dropped about twenty yards in front of me. Before I could dodge into the nearest grav-lift I was seized by at least half-a-dozen cops. They threw me into the can and piled in after me. I was hooked to a seat, and we jetted off.

I sat there and glowered at them.

"Aren't you going to ask what the charge is?" inquired one of them, grinning at me.

"That's the first thing they ask," said the fellow next to him, tapping his riot stick against his leg, and eyeing me professionally. "What's the charge, they always say. Don't you want to know what the charge is?"

"The only thing I've never been accused of," I said, "at one time or another, is murder on the high seas. Couldn't you make it that just this once? I'd like to add it to my collection."

"Sorry," said the one with the itchy stick hand, and they were all grinning now. "There's no charge for helping the police. Sometimes there's a little payment instead."

A few minutes later I was standing before the desk of Lieutenant John Simey, who was tall and spare, with piercing, grey eyes, and a hard, rasping voice. He looked me up and down. "Get him a chair," he said. "I don't know where all the chairs go to in this building. There are too many light-fingered cops about, that's what."

Someone brought a chair, the door closed, and we were

alone. "There's no need to make with the lights and the rubber truncheons," I told him. "I confess. Whatever it was, I did it. Sorry to deprive you of the innocent pleasure of half clubbing a man to death; but there it is. Shove the sheets over and I'll sign them."

I heard the door open again, and Benson's secretary came in. "Have you told him yet, Lieutenant?" she asked.

"You tell him," he shrugged. "He seems to think that I want to unload a crime sheet on him." A slight, predatory smile lit his harsh features. It was the smile on the face of the tiger, and innocent as I was it made me feel uneasy.

The blonde sat on the edge of the desk, casually swinging a shapely limb. "We wanted to thank you for that business of the safe," she said. "It was purely fortuitous I know; but it helped a great deal. You should keep this to yourself; but I've been trying to get a look inside that safe for months."

"You can rely on me," I said, winking. "Cops and robbers working together, eh? What an excellent idea. You should clean up."

Lieutenant Simey came to his feet. "What the hell are you implying?" he demanded.

"He was only joking," said the blonde. "I know him. He's a great joker. You were joking, weren't you?"

"Yes, of course," I said, with a forced smile. "Like she says, I'm a great joker. I've got the scars to prove it."

"I should blamed well think so," said the disgruntled officer, and sat down again. "Perhaps I'd better explain," he added, "that this young lady is one of our cleverest operatives, and is attached to the fraud squad. We've been investigating the affairs and business interests of Benson; but we lacked sufficient evidence to issue a general search warrant. We had to see what was in that safe before we could risk searching it officially. You gave us that opportunity, for which, naturally, we are pleased to extend our thanks.

Now it so happens that there is something else you can do for us, which is why I wanted you here in such a hurry."

"So you're a cop," I said to the girl.

She nodded. "Investigator Jane Mureau. Does that worry you?"

It worried me all right. It worried me a lot. It looked like the police had a new, secret weapon.

"What we want you to do for us is give us the lowdown on this rejuvenation racket that Benson was so interested in." Lieutenant Simey leant across the desk, and lowered his voice. "You work with us and I give you my solemn assurance that you won't be brought into it." He paused and looked at me.

So that was it, I thought. They didn't want to thank me at all, because there was nothing to thank me for. That safe hadn't yielded a blind thing. So now they wanted to indict him for fraud. It was the promotion stakes, of course.

"We have some evidence from a man named Swift," Simey continued. "Do you know him? He says that Benson made some very extravagant claims for these things he called rejuvenation globes."

"They worked, too," I said; "but whether they did or not you haven't got a leg to stand on as far as fraud is concerned. He never attempted to sell them."

"He's sold you down the river," the Lieutenant said quietly. "Did you know that. He wants to charge you and your friend Tetchum with fraud."

"And you don't want the tiddlers. You want the big fish?"

"You could put it that way."

"Maybe you think we didn't get anything from the safe," said Jane Mureau, with that jump in the dark that men call female intuition. "If so you're wrong. The thing is we didn't get enough. He's guilty all right, and we'll pin him in time; but it's going to be a long haul. We want something to frighten him with. Something to use as a lever. You know what I mean. We have to shake his confidence."

"What exactly did the globes do?" asked the Lieutenant. "If they did anything."

"They did one thing rather well," I said, and they leaned towards me. "You held the globe like this." There was a heavy, glass ash-tray on the desk. I picked it up. "Then you operated the switch. . . ."

"Yes?" said the Lieutenant interestedly.

"Well, I watched Benson do that very thing, and Benson, as you probably know, is rather thick around the middle. In fact, he has what Shakespeare referred to as a fair, round belly, if you'll excuse the term, although I wouldn't know if it is full capon lined or not. . . ."

Lieutenant Simey frowned at me. "What the hell are you talking about? I don't see where this is all leading."

"You will in a minute," I promised.

"Go on," said Jane Mureau. "He pressed the switch. What happened then?"

"His pants fell down," I said.

The Lieutenant shot back in his chair and flipped the intercom switch. "Johnson! Parkes!" he said in a choking voice. "Lieutenant Simey's office. Now!"

The two officers burst into the room and looked around. They must have thought he was being attacked.

Simey indicated me with a stabbing forefinger. "Throw him out," he said, "before I kill him!"

Investigator Jane Mureau had a tiny handkerchief jammed in her pretty mouth, and was shaking with suppressed laughter.

In the end four of them threw me out of the building. Taking an arm or a leg each they swung me back and forth a couple of times and then heaved together with such enthusiasm that I landed on the slow East pedestrip, and was carried away.

Later on I videoed Benson. He regarded me, blackly. "What the hell do you want?" he demanded. "Haven't the police caught up with you yet?"

"As a matter of fact," I said pleasantly, "I've just left Lieutenant John Simey. We had a nice little *tête-à-tête,* mostly about you. If you've missed any papers from your safe your ex-secretary's got them. You can probably have them back now that the photostatic copies have been filed."

His face had taken on a grey tinge. "So that was it," he said, and looked about him nervously. "How long have I got?" he whispered. "Why are you doing this, anyway?"

"I'm quixotic," I said, "and you've just about time to book to the Continent, and then beat it somewhere else on an earlier strato-jet, and under another name."

He nodded, and switched off.

Three weeks later I received a cable-order from Mexico for five hundred credits. It had been sent by a man named Smith. As I pointed out to Lieutenant John Simey that very afternoon, if it had been from Benson naturally I shouldn't have attempted to cash it; but three generations previously a member of the family had actually settled in Mexico, and he also had taken the name of Smith. So you see. . . .

"What did he do? Rob a bank?"

People are obsessed with banks these days. In point of fact he was arrested for some trifling misdemeanour like blowing up the local sewage works because he thought it was unhealthy. I forget the exact details.

He managed to blow up the County Jail as well, which was how he got away. I didn't tell the Lieutenant about this in case he had me thrown out again; but I did ask for the return of my money order. After all, one has to live.

They threw me out.

TWO'S COMPANY

by

JOHN RANKINE

Human relationships, especially between man and woman, have not often been handled sympathetically in science fiction—a subject matter which does not lend itself readily to such treatment—but new author John Rankine achieves this successfully in this story of a survey team temporarily stranded on an alien planet.

TWO'S COMPANY

THE black oval of the entry port diminished slowly to a dot and even in the thin atmosphere of Omega the definitive click of its closing could be heard from the edge of the clearway. Dag Fletcher, standing outside the main dome of the station, watched the silver arrow angle up for take off and saw the brilliant fan of orange flame build up before the noise and vibration shook the rock platform. Slowly, with a casual grace, *Interstellar-Two-Seven* began to lift and then flung itself into a streaking trajectory. In just under the ten seconds which Dag had automatically counted out to himself, it had dwindled away and the blue void was vacant and featureless as it had been through an eternity of time.

Even the long conditioning courses and the many previous missions could not prevent his feeling of loss and abandonment in this remote place. There was a tinge of regret too about the combination of chances which had sent him Meryl Wingard as assistant for the three month tour of duty. Not that there was anything wrong with the Wingard to look at. Far from it. She had elected to be moulded on the lines of Botticelli's Marine Venus and was as lovely as the original, but it seemed a meaningless beauty, since she worked with the inhumanity of a flawless machine. She was a mathematician of outstanding calibre and trained to a fantastic pitch of competence by years of single-minded effort.

The right person in every way for the mission, no doubt about that—with the banks of computers to keep tabs on; but not likely to add much gaiety to the long chore ahead. Moreover, he suspected that she had very little time for his sort of practical flair. As far as could be said of any spaceman reaching his rank, he was an improvisor, a lucky man, and an outside shot statistically speaking to be a Controller at all. Lean, tall, late thirties, with an easy relaxed slouch of a walk, he always stood out as an individual among the correct conservative types of the Senior personnel.

He moved back into the airlock and flipped switches to drop the outer atmosphere shield. A green glow showed the seal complete and he put the regulator to Robot and let the automatic gear carry on.

Meryl was not in the communal living space, so he moved on into the Controller's suite. He had settled in there in the week that the ship had remained to do those jobs which needed the full crew. Now he shrugged out of his spacesuit and the moulded rubber inner suit and took a shower. Then he dressed for comfort in slacks, sneakers, and a gaudy Tee-shirt.

The suite was built in a sixty-foot pressurized dome divided by two diameter walls into two small and two large arcs. Large—dayroom and bedroom; small—bathroom and store. The dayroom was dominated by a scanner on a platform against the outer wall. Dag stepped up to it and looked without much enthusiasm at the panoramic view of the planet endlessly presented on the flat screen. He tuned for the immediate area of the space station and a tract of some square miles was presented with crystal clarity. Typical of the planet was the mixture of rocky plateau and wide shallow valley filled with thick yellow-green vegetation. The station was set on a half-mile square platform which had been ground to a perfect level. It made one of the best space ports in the galaxy and served a six dome main station. Ten smaller robot stations dotted the planet and must each be visited once in the three month tour. In theory at least nothing could go wrong with them; but their computer programmes had to have a quarterly check since even tiny errors could drift into serious chaos given long enough.

The project on Omega was to produce an earth type atmosphere. Already the oxygen level was one quarter earth and in two years it should be fully habitable. Gravity at ·72 earth was an attractive feature and the planet was sure to be high on the list for future colonists. A dull place though, reflected Fletcher, with its never ending ravines and tumbled rock table lands—though its appearance would improve when a balanced atmosphere produced rain and cloud and stretches of water.

He left the scanner and returned to reception. Still no sign of the girl; so he ate alone, pressing labelled switches which delivered heated foods to the service hatch in the dining alcove. As he finished his coffee and lit a cigarette, she came in, still wearing the close-fitting inner skin of her spacesuit—a silver sheath—which stressed every line of a perfect figure. Her fair hair was straight and almost shoulder length and swung as she moved like a pale gold elastic bell. The blue and yellow rank flashes on the right shoulder were only half a bar less than his own; but she was as correct in address as if she were straight from training school and they used speech automatically, where others in this situation might have got down at once to the more intimate thought transfer.

"Controller, there's a drift in Station 9. I should be glad if we could make that our first visit."

"Check. You comfortable in your cubby hole?" He had not asked before in the busy days of take over.

"Thank you, yes; but if you don't mind I'll use the lounge here to work in. I prefer a large free space when possible."

He could sympathize with this view and wondered how she had felt in the cramped living-room of the spaceship. But he kept this thought out of the transfer area of his mind.

Dag looked at the model globe of Omega and spun it to find Station 9. It was about 200 earth miles distant—a two hour journey in one of the Centre's hover cars. Days on Omega were relatively short, being only 15½ earth hours. It was now about two hours to nightfall and although, eventually, earth personnel drifted out of phase with this time scheme, it was still convenient to talk about "today" and "tomorrow".

"Tomorrow, then? One hour after first light."

"Check. I'll say Good night, Controller."

"Good night."

Her detachment was complete and there was no pose in it. A cool madame there, he thought—but probably it meant more positive success for the mission, he would have nothing to take his mind off the job. However, he recognized that he was slightly piqued at her lack of interest in him and after serving himself with a small whisky from the bar, he returned to his own rooms.

It was brilliantly light when they came out of the airlock and crossed the forecourt. Fletcher decided to take the middle range car and wound back its pressure sealed roof. He made a routine check of the cylinder rack and they climbed in. They fastened seat belts and at zero power the car edged out from the parking canopy. In the open, Dag lifted her in a smooth sharp climb to maximum height and then set the automatic pilot to home on Station 9 at full power. The car hovered and then slowly turned until it was exactly on the beam path and then moved away with effortless acceleration.

The surface of Omega unrolled before them, visible through the wide screen and the transparent floor. Rocky plateau and valley in succession endlessly. Valleys choked to their rocky confines with the crawling yellow-green plant life. It was by the controlled decomposition of this that the atmosphere was being created. The break down would have a two-fold purpose, oxygen and nitrogen given off and the ground cleared for the future settlers. As they neared the sub-station, the effects of the work made a dramatic change in the scenery. There was a succession of completely clear valleys where the bare ground showed deep purple. Then the station itself could be seen. Three large domes and a small port.

They swept down to a perfect landing and climbed out on to the apron. In minutes they were through the airlock and inside the main dome. Meryl only paused to hinge back her helmet and crossed directly to the control console. All such stations were built to a familiar plan and she quickly identified the essential elements. She switched out the robot computer control and took it on manual. With high speed calculations she monitored the system for five minutes, then switched back.

"There's been a drift in the computer setting. I'll have to work back on this."

"How much time do you need?"

"Two hours certainly. Possibly two and a half." This would be cutting it fine if they decided to return before dark. They could stay overnight, of course—there was food and accommodation for several months if necessary; but they both preferred to get back to the relative comfort of the main station.

"See how it goes."

"Right."

The pale gold head bent over the horizontal presentation table and long detailed equations were pencilled on the ivorine monitoring panels. He followed the processes for a few minutes then she lost him with a piece of mathematical short circuiting which was outside his range. He certainly had a first class assistant and he admitted to himself that the job would have taken him several days.

"I'll take a look outside." There was no reply; she was completely absorbed in the work.

The lock for exit was a complete manual and it was ten minutes before he stood beside the car. He took her up to fifty feet and made a sweeping circuit of the immediate area. The nearest valleys were clear of growth and showed like purple lakes. The dark powdery soil was high in fertility and would make ideal farm land. Four valleys were under ray bombardment and beginning to show patches of clear ground. The ray apparatus was set up and moved by a full crew at each visit of the spaceship and monitored in the interval by the computers in the sub-stations.

He set the car down in one of the cleared areas and took a soil sample in a specimen jar from the rack above the landing skid. He read the fix from the car's navigation table and marked the sample with date, time, and location. The base analysts were assembling a detailed report on every valley and a complete farming plan would be made before one colonist set foot on the planet. It was median time and exactly half the short day had gone. By the time he had re-admitted himself to the dome it was median plus a half and Meryl was drinking coffee.

"How does it go?"

"No problem. The fault wasn't hard to find; but I'll need to test run for about half an hour to make sure that the deviation has been cleared."

"Fine. If we move at five we shall be back before dark."

He took time to inspect the plant. It was unlikely that they would have time to pay a second visit; so he initialled and dated the check tablets at each section. It was almost three months to the day since the previous Controller had done the same.

At median plus one and a half she signalled "job complete", and after the routine tests of equipment, they re-entered the waiting car. Fletcher felt that he must give due credit for her success.

"Thank you for that. Not many people could have straightened it out in the time."

The reply was typical. "Not at all. Any competent mathematician could have done it." But he sensed that she was pleased to be complimented and he wondered if a better relationship might not be possible between them.

On the return, he took control on manual and pushed the speed above the range of the automatic pilot. This should bring them in in daylight. Navigation would be unaffected by darkness, but even the few moments of transfer from car to dome could be unpleasant in the intense cold of the night temperature on Omega.

They were under two miles from base, with the homing beam filling the scanner with a pathway like a red carpet unrolled in welcome, when the car defied statistical likelihood and broke its maker's record for complete reliability. It was so quickly done that it was impossible to remember what in fact had happened. Dag eased down to landing speed and switched in the robot pilot. The car lost height and then began to pick up speed in a tearing near vertical dive. There was a splintering crash. Where the screen had been was the scratched face of living rock. This Dag saw before he blacked out and sagged down against the harness which alone had kept his head from the incoming splinters.

He carried into oblivion also a flash picture of the girl strained against the strap with her hair streaming forward like a shining pennant.

Minutes later he climbed back into consciousness and the shifting blur settled to hard factual pictures of a situation as bad as it could be. Pain needled him to full awareness and he moved cautiously. Nothing seemed broken, but a rock fragment had torn through his spacesuit below the left knee and the quilted sections above had constricted to form an emergency air seal. There was a slow ooze of blood through the torn fabric. Looking across at the girl, he stabbed, swearing, at the release catch of his harness and heaved himself out of his bucket seat. She was out cold—as he had been; but there was a pallor about her skin which was ominous. A spur of rock had thrust in at head level on her side and had punctured the helmet of her suit. Since the car was no longer pressurized, she was at surface pressure for Omega and was breathing Omega atmosphere. The suit's cylinders had emptied quickly in a vain effort to build up against the leak. She was in the same state as an almost drowned man and Dag knew that it was a matter of minutes and some luck if he could do anything at all about it.

He jabbed open her harness release and heaved her on to the sloping floor of the rear compartment. Stripping off the broken suit he looked along the rack of spares for something near the size. Even working at speed, he registered the light strength she had, the perfectly modelled knees and ankles and high round breasts. He zipped off his own helmet and clipped in the emergency air line to face mask. He filled his own lungs with an oxygen plus mixture and, using mouth to mouth respiration technique, made her breathe. He worked steadily for two minutes and was beginning to feel the strain of it, when her eyelids moved.

He put the mask over her mouth and nose and pulled forward his own helmet, glad to get air without conscious effort. Grabbing the suit he had earmarked, he set the air flow to its helmet then slipped it over her head. She was fully aware now and had taken in the situation. Quickly he slipped her legs into the new suit and she kneeled forward to help. Within half a minute pressure was normal and a more natural colour had returned to her skin.

Dag picked out a replacement suit for himself and

realized how groggy he felt. For himself, he reversed the process and fitted the new helmet first; then as he was peeling off the old trousers he felt the snag in the left leg and remembered why he was changing at all. As he did a complicated jack-knife to keep the supply of gas to the new suit and free the old, he felt her hand on his shoulder—"Let me help." She had broken out a first aid kit and poured some solvent on the sticky mess below the knee.

"This needs a stitch. I can take care of it."

She did a quick but careful bit of surgery with the sterile instruments in the pack, and then a dressing. He shrugged into the suit and stood up to inspect the damage.

Time was running badly against them. Very little daylight remained and unless they were to freeze to death something must be done to patch up the car. He moved gingerly back into the pilot seat. The floor was broken and jammed on to a jagged rock splinter and a narrow fracture spread back into the body of the car. The power pack had been crumpled into the cab and fissures crossed the panoramic screen in every direction. There were two plastic spray containers in the repair locker and some sheets of white plastic. It was intended to make a temporary seal when any part of the fabric was punctured by meteoritic fragments. It might just do—used sparingly. She was already stripping the packaging off a container and he realized that they had dropped easily and naturally into thought transfer. He smiled thanks and got to work.

The rock seemed solid and free from porous pumice. He began sealing the broken edges of the car to the floor, making the intrusive splinters an integral part of the skin. The plastic sprayed out under pressure and set on contact. The whole of the front was complete when the first cylinder hissed empty. They were within minutes of the short twilight.

The cabin floor lightened as he turned to work on it and

he saw that she had fitted two hand torches by suction clips to the rear bulkhead. Now that there was time to look at each other, she allowed maximum penetration of her mind for some seconds. He was aware of calm acceptance of the likelihood of death, no hint of criticism, concern for himself, and a sense of comradeship. Reciprocally, he dissolved his own thought barrier and she was conscious of his gratitude for her help, and a new element of personal admiration.

The second cylinder completed a seal for the floor and he looked round for other punctures. There were some minor ones which he first plugged and then sprayed. Using a spare suit cylinder he built up pressure inside the wreck and then set up an air conditioning circuit. It was now dark and with the dark the cold began. The surrounding rocks began to cool rapidly, making sharp cracking noises like breaking sticks.

They were able to take off their helmets and make a scratch meal. An inspection of the lockers produced biscuit and self-heating soup. The cars had little food stock, only spare air bottles being regarded as vital.

Now the cold began to be a thing to reckon with. Moved by the logic of circumstances they made one narrow sleeping bag out of every available bit of fabric with the seat cushions as mattress. Still wearing their inner suits, but not needing helmets in the stabilized atmosphere, they squeezed in and lay still. Dag turned her towards him until they were pressed together from knees to shoulders. Her nipples were noticeably firm against his chest and her perfume was exhilarating. If they got out of this he knew he would want to love this girl, but he knew also that this was not the time and he touched her hair with his lips and said good night.

They slept fitfully for six hours before the cold dug down into them. Dag moved stiffly and a gossamer web of ice crystals tinkled and cracked round his head. He squeezed her shoulders gently and as she woke said "Two hours to daylight—we could do with some warmth."

The air of the cabin was biting cold and their nest of fabric had hardened into an inflexible carapace. Ice ribbed the tubular cross members. Dag levered himself partly out and reached over for the last two cans of soup. He checked an exclamation of pain as he touched the cold metal and found that the tins were anchored to the floor by a rim of ice. She added her grip to his and they wrenched them free. Bashing the striker's against the floor triggered them off. The heat melted the ice near the tins and made a pool of water; but the soup was hot and its warmth spread through their bodies.

It was not easy to sleep again and they began to talk about the careers which had led them to this point of time. He found she had an unexpected fund of humour. This added another dimension to the expert mathematician. They strained close together to keep in every fugitive calory. The cold thrust down into them and it was a race between dawn and a freezing death. They held on.

Dawn came on Omega in a dramatic racing flash and filled the cabin with a harsh neon-like glow. The rapidly rising heat turned their bed into a sodden heap as the ice melted away. The walls streamed with released condensation too fast for the balancer to adjust.

Dag pushed her damp hair aside and with a hand on either side of her face kissed her mouth.

"We have eight hours. There will not be another chance."

She nodded and, copying his gesture, kissed him in the same way. Then she stood up and touched the release studs at the neck of her suit and zipped down the front panel. Then she peeled it off and took a pad of rough cleaning tissues and began a brisk massaging rub. Dag took another pad and scrubbed her back. He did the same himself and with blood circulating freely and feeling ready to tackle the day, they dressed again in complete spacesuits.

Dag broke out the emergency exit and they crawled through on to the rock. The lip of the ravine was about fifty yards away and the domes of the station seemed near enough to touch on the far side of the valley. But eight hours was too small an allowance of time to do a tricky rock climb of eighty feet into the valley, cut through about a mile of tangled vegetation, and climb the opposite cliff. There would have to be another way.

"Get out the spare suits and any rope you can find," and as she edged back into the wrecked car, he walked quickly to the top of the cliff and looked across. Almost in the centre of the valley was a low outcrop of rock showing like a black stain on the grey-green carpet. Meryl had brought out two lengths of nylon rope and the spare suits and he ran back to help her carry them. Even with reduced gravity it was a good load among the crazy rocks and they were glad to pile it at the edge.

Meryl could see no hope of crossing in time and he could feel her mind reluctantly preparing for defeat. Dag found her work to do.

"Inflate a spare suit and tie a rope to the centre of the front harness."

As she worked on it he went on, "What do you say is the distance to that black rock and what rocket charge would send an empty suit to it with a trailing rope?"

The variables made it a tricky calculation. He had made his own rough estimate; but he could do with the best approximation that could be made. There was low gravity, the drag effect of the increasing length of rope, the effectiveness of different rocket charges, and the behaviour of an inflated suit to think of. It took five minutes of calculation before she said "Five-eighths charge and a launching angle of thirty-seven degrees." He accepted this without question though his own effort had produced a higher angle for the launch.

"Right."

He twisted out one of the two small rocket canisters from his belt. They were for use in zero weight as propulsion for a short trip outside a stationary ship. They would not move a man on Omega even with its reduced gravity. But they might serve to move a balloon. He spread-eagled the inflated suit on the rocks and carefully sighted along the back to line it up with the target, then he raised the head on a cairn of small stones checking to an angle of 37 degrees with his wrist watch. Then he slotted the charge canister into the empty sheath in the centre of the shoulder straps. He turned the charge indicator to five-eighths and stood aside with the firing toggle in his hand. This was it. If it worked they were halfway home. He pulled the cord gently so as not to disturb the setting of the light figure.

The suit took off looking like a man in space and rose swiftly to the height of its trajectory and then began a homing descent to the rock with the thin nylon line snaking out behind. From where they stood it seemed certain that their projectile would overshoot. Then the increasing check of the trailing rope snatched it down from its soaring curve to a straight line drop and the suit disappeared in a tangle of rock. The rope was immensely strong; but could fray and cut. Dag hauled back until he felt it wedge firmly between two craggy projections, then made fast at their end.

He made a tight bundle of their remaining spares and attached it to a short length of line which he looped over the rope and then sent it like a miniature cable car shooting across the valley. It disappeared into the rocks and he began to work out a braking device with a slipping knot which could be jerked to tighten on the leading rope. When he was satisfied, he showed the girl how it worked and said:

"You next—if the line wears through it will be with me and you will have to sort it out for both of us."

She stood at the edge of the cliff, gripped the two trailing cords and stepped out over the drop. The perfect lieutenant, he thought, as he followed the dizzy speed of her descent. No questions or argument; but maximum efficient help. Even the bulky outer suit could not completely disguise the slim silver figure. The sag of the rope slowed her a little near the rock and she seemed to be managing the improvised brake. Then she was down in a stumbling run and he saw the small distant figure raise an arm in signal.

Unhesitating he swung out himself with the query—third time lucky?—in his mind. Near the rock he saw that his greater weight was sagging the rope below the rim of the rock outcrop and as he used all his strength to brake on the rope, he had to lift his legs in a full knee bend to fend off. The jar of impact almost broke his grip; but she was there lying out along the rope to help him in.

The next stage was clearer now and they looked silently at it for some minutes. Their final objective was higher than the rock they were on and they could not hope to make it in a toiling hand over hand climb. The best they could do would be to repeat their performance and slide down to the scree at the foot of the cliff and work out the next step from there.

She began another careful calculation of distances and velocities and once more they spreadeagled the inflated suit. Direction was not so critical for this shot into a wide target area and they saw it hit the cliff face and drop back into the scree. Dag pulled in cautiously and the suit dragged about twenty yards before it wedged. They went into the same routine and soon they were standing together at the foot of the last barrier.

Even under the low gravity of Omega they were feeling the physical strain, and as they scrambled up the last of the scree to the sheer wall of the cliff, Dag saw no way of beating the clock and getting to the plateau in the two hours of daylight left to them. Any lengthy exploration to left or right for a reasonable climb was out for a start, and in any case the cliff was uniformly sheer as far as could be seen. The spaceport apron had been given a mathematically even surface to the very edge of the cliff and visualizing the surface above, he could think of nothing immediately above them likely to anchor a rope. Some sort of tined grapnel might do—but made with what?

He broke the container of his anti-hostility pack and took out the small laser pistol—reflecting that if they ever got back to the dome this would need an explanatory section to itself in the station log. He beamed it at the cliff edge and small fragments powdered down. Given several days he might have cut steps with the intense narrow beam : but he did not have days.

"What charges are left?"

"Two complete and two part used."

"Would they do a demolition job?"

"Properly placed it could move this cliff."

The half formed idea clarified in his mind and he aimed directly at the sheer rock at about shoulder level. The face began to crumble in an area about the size of a cent piece, as the ray burned into it. He shifted an inch and bored again and after thirty minutes he had excavated a hole about eighteen inches deep and about two inches in diameter. Into this he packed one rocket canister with a thin twist of nylon line on its release toggle. Then he tamped home fragments of stone, only leaving movement for the cord.

They went back into the scree paying out line, and selected cover between two heavy boulders. In a single movement he jerked the trigger and flung himself down beside her with his arm over her shoulders. In their silent world, the noise seemed immense and debris crumbled down in a sliding rush. When movement stopped they stood up.

A tall oblong of the cliff face had come away and shattered like a slab of glass hit with a sledge-hammer. Angular fantastic fragments leaned forward to the new level and a jagged rangle led almost to the top. What problem there would be in that last step could only be assessed when they got there and they began to climb.

Some steps could only be gained by team work. Meryl climbed on his shoulders and got a finger-tip hold on a ledge, then he lifted her feet and she heaved herself on to the level. Then she made a belay and he climbed slowly to join her.

The last step was the highest yet and it was only by standing on his fully outstretched hands that she got a finger hold. It was a slow painful grind to bend her weary muscles and finally lever herself over the top. She lay forward, face downwards, sobbing with exhaustion. Waiting for the rope to snake down to him, he saw that they were within minutes of the twilight. Then he was beside her and with one arm across her shoulders they began a clumsy run to the nearest dome.

They were twenty yards from the lock when the light began to go and as he pulled down the opening lever, the blackness was complete. He felt her slipping down beside him and had to hold her as the door swung in to receive them. With one last effort he picked her up and carried her into the light and warmth.

The few minutes' rest while the robot mechanism adjusted pressures, gave him time to recover and he was able to carry her through into her room when the inner door opened for them. He took off her outer suit and put her on her bed. She was asleep and breathing deeply and easily.

He walked slowly to his own suite and stripped off and took a shower. It seemed a long time since he had last stood there and it was wonderful to feel the sweat and dust sluicing away and taking aches and tiredness with it. He even smoked a cigarette at intervals dodging the deluge. Then he took time to dress and wondered whether or not to wake her for a meal.

Still debating, he went out to the dining area to fix himself a drink. The table was already set for two and the food was ready. She came out from her room. She was wearing the ceremonial tabard of green and gold caught at the sides with bronze clasps. Her hair was combed down almost to her shoulders and swung like an elastic golden bell as she moved.

She said, "Welcome aboard, Controller," and he knew that the rest of the tour was not going to be any problem at all.

MAN ON BRIDGE

by

BRIAN W. ALDISS

Here is a rather grim little story with overtones of Orwell's 1984, *in which Brian W. Aldiss deals with the coming of* Homo superior—*but not as the type of superman we would expect. Mr. Aldiss, undoubtedly Britain's foremost science fiction author at the moment, is noted for his off-trail and often macabre approaches to futuristic themes.*

MAN ON BRIDGE

VIEW sliding down out of the west-moving clouds, among the mountains, to the roads that halt at the barbed wire. Sight of electrified fences, ray gun posts on stilts, uniformed guards, readily familiar to any inhabitant of this continent for the last two hundred, three hundred years. Sun comes out on to dustbins and big slosh buckets behind low cookhouse; guards cuddle rifles, protecting cookhouse and slosh buckets. Flies unafraid of rifles.

Chief living thing in camp: man. Many of them walking or being marched between buildings, which are long-established without losing air of semi-permanence. The inhabitants of this camp have an identification mark which merely makes them anonymous. On their backs is stuck a big yellow C.

C for Cerebral, yellow as prole-custard.

C for Cerebral, a pleasant splash of brains against the monochrome of existence.

A group of C's pushing a cart of refuse over to the tip, conversing angrily. . . .

"Nonsense, Megrip, methadone hydrachloride may be a powerful analgesic, but its use would be impossible in those circumstances, because it would set up an addiction."

"Never liked the ring of that word analgesic. . . ."

"Even postulating addiction, even postulating addiction, I still say——"

The wind blows, the cart creaks.

More C's, swabbing latrines, four of them in dingy grey, talking as the C's always talk, because they have joy in talking and wrangling. Never forget that this is a report of happiness, following the dictum of the great prole-leader,

Keils: however much he may appear to suffer, the C is inwardly happy as long as he is permitted to talk freely; with cerebrals, debate replaces the natural prole urges such as action and drinking and procreation. These C's conversing airily in the jakes. . . .

"No, what we are witnessing today are the usual after-effects of any barbarian invasion: the decline of almost all standards causes the conquered race to turn in despair to extremes of vice. This isn't the first time Europe has had to suffer the phenomenon, God knows."

"That would be feasible enough, Jeffers, if there had indeed been an invasion." This one talks intelligently, but through a streaming cold.

"The intelligent have been overwhelmed by the dull. Is not that an invasion?"

"More, I would say, of a self-betrayal, in that——"

Unison flushing of twenty closets drowns sound of cranky voices. The situation is analysed shrewdly enough; they mistake in thinking that analysis is sufficient, and swab contentedly in the grey water round their ankles.

Sun returning fitfully again. It penetrates a drab, damp camp room where stand three men. Two are anxious at their approaching visit to the camp commander. One is indifferent to the universe, for he has had half his brain removed. They call him Adam X. He can: stand, sit, lie down, eat, and defecate when reminded to do so; he has no habits. One of the other two men, Morgern Grabowicz, thinks Adam X is free, while the other, Jon Winther, regards him as dead.

Adam stands there while the other two argue over him. Sometimes changes of expression steal over his face, gentle smiles, sadnesses, extreme grimaces, all coming and going gradually, as the part of his brain that is left slyly explores territory that belongs to the part of his brain that is gone. The smiles have no relation to the current situation; nor have the sadnesses; both are entirely manifestations of his nervous system.

The chief intelligence behind the complex system of operations Adam has undergone is Grabowicz, cold and clever old Grabowicz. Winther was involved at every stage, but in a subordinate role. In long months and mazes of delirium, Adam has been where they could not follow. Now Adam is newly out of bed, and Roban Trabann, the camp commander, is prepared to take an interest in his maimed existence.

Grabowicz and Winther wish to converse with Adam, but as yet conversation is not possible in their meaning of the word. Jon Winther bears the C on his back with an air. He should have been a prole rather than a cerebral, for he has the warmth. He has kept the warmth because he sometimes sees his family, which is solid-prole. The other man, the older, is Morgern Grabowicz, brought here from Styria: hard, cunning, cold, should have two C's on his back. He made Adam X.

Adam X was once just another young C, born Adran Zatrobik, until Grabowicz began the operations on his brain, whittling it away, a slice here, a whole lobe there . . . carving the man himself, until he made Adam X.

Grabowicz is looking remote and withdrawn now, as some C's will when they are angry, instead of letting the true emotion show. Winther is speaking to him in a low voice, also angry. Their voices are relayed to the camp commander because the electricians have finally got the microphones going again in Block B. Two years they have been out of order, despite the highest priority for attention. There are too many cogs in the clumsy machine. The two C's have observed the electricians at work, but are indifferent to what is overheard.

Winther is talking.

"You know why he wants to see us, Morgern. Trabann is

no fool. He is going to ask us to make more men like Adam X, and we can't do that."

Grabowicz replies: "As you say, Jon, Trabann is no fool—therefore he will see that we can make more men like Adam. What has once been done can be done again."

Winther replies: "But he doesn't care what happens to any C, or to anyone, for that matter. In your heart, you know that what we have done to Adam is to commit murder, and we cannot do it again!"

"In your descent into melodrama, you neglect a couple of points in logic. First, I care no more than Trabann what is to be the fate of any individual, since I believe the human race to be superfluous; it fulfils no purpose. Secondly, since Adam lives, he cannot be murdered within the legal definition of the term. Thirdly, I say as I have before, that if Trabann gives us the facilities, we can very easily repeat our work, this time improving greatly on the prototype. And fourthly——"

"Morgern, I beg of you, don't go on! Don't make yourself into something as inhuman as we have made Adam! I've only been your friend here for so long because I know that within you there is someone who suffers as much as—and for—the rest of us. . . . Drop this stupid estranged attitude! We don't want to collaborate with proles, even gifted ones like Trabann, and we know—you know, that Adam represents our failure, not our success."

Grabowicz paced about the room. When he replied, his voice came distantly.

"You should have been a prole yourself," he told his friend, in that cold, flat voice, still without anger. "You have lost the scientific spirit, or you would know that it is still too early to use emotive words like 'success' or 'failure' of our experiment here. Adam is an unknown factor as yet. Nor have scientists ever been morally responsible for the results of their work, any more than the engineer is responsible for the vehicles that collide on the bridge he has built. As to your claim on what you call friendship between us, that can only be based on respect, and in your case——"

"You feel nothing!" Jon Winther exclaims. "You are as dead as Adam X!"

Listening to this argument, Commander Trabann is interested to hear a C using the very accusation the Prole Party brings against all the C's. Since the world's C's were segregated in camps, the rest of the world has run much more smoothly—or run *down* much more smoothly, you may prefer to say—and the terrible rat-race known to both the old communist and capitalist blocks as "progress" has given way to the truly democratic grandeur of the present staticist utopia, where not only all men but all intelligences are equal.

Now Grabowicz speaks to Adam, saying, "Are you ready to go and meet the camp commandant, Adam?"

"I am fully prepared, and await the order to move." Adam's voice is a light one, almost female, but with a slight throatiness. He rarely looks at the men he addresses.

"Are you feeling well this morning, Adam?"

"You will observe that I am standing up. That is to accustom myself to the fits of dizziness to which I am subject. Otherwise, I have no feelings in my body."

Winther says: "Does your head ache, Adam?"

"By my body I implied my whole anatomy. I have no headache."

To Grabowicz, Winther says: "An absence of headache! He makes it sound like a definition of happiness!"

Ignoring his assistant, Grabowicz asks Adam, "Did you dream last night, Adam?"

"I dreamed one dream, of five minutes duration."

"Well, go on then, man. I have told you before to be alert for the way several following questions may be inferred from a lead question."

"I recall that, Morgern," Adam says meekly, "but I supposed that we were waiting for the signal to leave this room and go to the commander's office. The answer to what I judge your implied question to be is that I dreamed of a bench."

"Ah, that's interesting! You see, Jon? And what was this bench like?"

Adam says: "It had a steel support at each end. It was perfectly smooth and unmarked. I think it stood on a polished floor."

"And what happened?"

"I dreamed of it for five minutes."

Winther says: "Didn't you sit down on the bench?"

Adam: "I was not present in my dream."

Winther: "What happened?"

Adam: "Nothing happened. There was just the bench."

Grabowicz: "You see, Jon! Even his dreams are chemically clean! We have eradicated all the old muddle of hypothalamus and the visceral areas of the brain. You have here your first purely cerebral man. Putting sentiment aside, you can see what our next task is; we must persuade Trabann to let us have, say, three male C's and three female. They will all undergo the same treatment that Adam has done, and we then segregate them—it will need much co-operation from Trabann and his bosses, of course—and let them breed and rear their children free from outside interference. The result will be the beginning of a clique dominated by pure intellect."

"They'd be incapable of breeding!" Winther said disgustedly. "By by-passing Adam's visceral brain, we've deprived him of half his autonomic nervous system. He could no more make love than fly!"

Then the guards came shouting, cursing the three C's out of their refuge of words into the real world of hard fact.

Patched boots on the patched concrete. On the distant

mountains, sunshine, lingering, then sweeping down toward the town of Saint Praz, below the camp. Sky almost all blue. Adam X walking carefully among them, looking at the ground to keep his balance as he was marched to the office.

Trabann makes a good camp commander. Not only is he formidably ugly, he has some pretentions of being "brainy", and so is jealous of the two thousand C's under him, and treats them accordingly.

All the while Grabowicz is delivering his report, Trabann sits glaring at Adam X, his bulbous nose shining over the bristles of his moustache. Of course, Trabann can come to no decision: everything must be passed on to his superiors: but he does his best to look like a man about to come to a decision, as he stirs and shuffles inside his heavy clothes.

While Winther stands by, Grabowicz does most of the talking, going into lengthy technical details of the surgery, and quoting from his notes. Trabann becomes bored, ceasing to listen since this is all being recorded on a tape machine by a secretary. He becomes more interested when Grabowicz puts forward his idea for creating more men and women like Adam and trying to breed from them. Breeding Trabann understands, or at least the crude mechanics of it.

Finally, Trabann examines Adam X, speaking to him, and questioning him. Then he purses his lips and says slowly to Grabowicz, "What you did, told in plain language, is wipe out this man's subconscious."

Grabowicz replies: "Don't give me that antiquated freudian nonsense. I mean, sir, that the body of theoretic work incorporating the idea of the subconscious mind was discontinued over a century ago. At least, in the C camps it was."

Trabann makes a note that once Grabowicz has served his purpose he undergoes treatment B35, or even B38. He sharply dismisses Grabowicz, who is marched off protesting, while Jon Winther and Adam X are made to stay. Trabann considers Winther a useful man for making trouble among C's themselves; he has some prole features, despite such typical Cerebral habits as habitual use of forbidden past and future tenses in his speech.

Trabann says to Winther: "Suppose we are breeding these purely intellectual children, are they Cerebrals or Proles?"

Winther: "Neither. They will be new people, if they can be bred. I have my doubts about that."

Trabann: "But *if* they are bred—they are on your side?"

Winther: "Who can say? You are thinking of something twenty years ahead."

Trabann: "You are trying to trap me, for you know that such thinking is treasonable. It is not for a prisoner to trap his commandant."

Winther, shrugging his shoulders: "You know why I am a prisoner—because the laws are so stupid that we prefer to break them than live by them, although it means lifelong imprisonment."

Trabann: "For that retort, distorting reality of world situation, an hour's D90 afterwards. You can admit to me freely that you and all C's wish to rule the world."

Winther: "Need we have that one again?"

The guards are summoned to administer the D90 on the spot. Before it is carried out, Winther defiantly claims Cerebrals more capable of governing well than what he terms "anti-intellectuals". He adds that C's undergo much of what they suffer as a sort of self-imposed discipline, since they believe that one must serve to rule. So again we meet this dangerous C heresy, first formulated in the forty-fifth chapter of the prime work of our great master Keils. How wise he was to categorize this belief that dominance lies through servitude as "extreme cerebral terrorism".

When the D90 is over, Adam X is given a few blows across the face, and the two C's are dismissed and returned to the square.

That day, Trabann works long over his report. Dimly, he senses great potential. He does not understand what Adam X can do. He gets bored with the effort of trying to think, and is unhappy because he knows thinking, or at least "thinking-to-a-purpose" is on the black list of party activities.

But, two nights later, Camp Commander Trabann is much more happy. The local militia bring him a document written by the C, Jon Winther, that tells Trabann things he feels his superiors desire to know. It tells them certain things about Adam's abilities. He passes it on with a memorandum expressing his detestation at the cerebral attitudes expressed in the manuscript. Here follows the Winther manuscript, which begins as Winther is recovering from the administration of the D90 already mentioned.

There was a long period when I lay between consciousness and unconsciousness, aware only of the palsy in my body (Jon Winther writes). They had injected the mouth of a quick-vacuum pump into one of my arteries and sucked all my blood from my body, syphoning it rapidly back again as I fell senseless. What finally drew my attention away from the jarring of my bruised heart was the sound of Adam X, breathing heavily near me.

I rolled myself over on to my stomach and looked at him. His nose was still bleeding slightly, his face and clothes disfigured with blood.

When he saw me looking at him, he said, "I do not wish to live, Jon."

I don't want to hate them, but I hated them when I looked at Adam; and I hated our side too, for Adam could be reckoned a collaboration between the two sides. "Wipe your face, Adam," I said. He was incapable even of thinking of doing that for himself.

We lay about in a stupor of indifference until a guard came and told us it was time to move. Shakily, I got to my feet and helped Adam up. We moved outside, into warm and welcome afternoon sun.

"Time's so short and so long," I said. I was light-headed; even at the time, the words sounded foolish. But feeling that sun, I knew myself to be a living organism and blessed with a consciousness that lasted but a flash yet often seemed, subjectively, to be the burden of eternity.

Adam stood woodenly by me and said without changing his expression, "You see life as a contrast between misery and pleasure, Jon; that is not a correct interpretation."

"It's a pretty good rule of thumb, I should have thought."

"Thought and non-thought is the only valid line of comparison."

"Bit of a bird's eye view, isn't it? That puts us on the same level as the proles."

"Exactly."

Suddenly angry, I said, "Look, Adam, let me take you home. I'd like to get you away from the camp atmosphere. My sisters can look after us for a few hours. Knowing Trabann, I think there's a pretty good chance the guard will let us through the gates."

"They will not let me through because I am a specimen."

"When Trabann is not sure what to do, he likes a bit of action."

When he nodded indifferently, I took his arm and led him towards the gates. It was always an ordeal, moving towards those great slab-cheeked guards, so contemptuous of eye, so large in their rough uniforms and boots, as they stood there holding their rifles like paddles. We produced our identity sticks, which were taken from us, and were allowed to pass, and go through the side-gate, between the strands of barbed wire, into the free world outside.

"They enjoy their show of might," Adam said. "These people have to express their unhappiness by using ugly things like guns and ill-fitting uniforms, and the whole conception of the camp."

"We are unhappy, but we don't find that sort of thing necessary."

"No, Jon, I am not unhappy. I just feel empty and do not wish to live."

His talk was full of that sort of conversation-stopper.

We strode down the road at increasing pace as the way steepened between cliffs. The ruined spires and roofs of the town were rising out of the dip ahead, and I wanted only to get home; but since I had never caught Adam in so communicative a frame of mind, I felt I had to take advantage of it and find out what I could from him.

"This not wishing to live, Adam—this is just post-operational depression. When it wears off, you will recover your spirits."

"I think not. I have no spirits. Morgern Grabowicz cut them away. I can only reason, and I see that there is no point to life but death."

"That I repudiate with all my heart. On the contrary, while there is life, there is no death. Even now, with all my limbs aching from that filthy prole punishment, I rejoice in every breath I take, and in the effect of the light on those houses, and the crunch of this track under our feet."

"Well, Jon, you must be allowed your simple vegetable responses." He spoke with such finality that my mouth was stopped.

The little town of Saint Praz is just above the line of the vine, though the brutal little river Quviv that cuts the town in two goes hurtling down to water the vineyards only ten kilometres away. The bridge that spans the Quviv marks the beginning of Saint Praz; next to it stands the green-domed church of Saint Praz And The Romantic Agony, and next to the church is the street in which the remains of my family live. As we climbed its cobbled way, I saw my sister Bynca leaning out of the upper window, talking to someone below. We went into the house, and Bynca ran to welcome me with cries of delight.

"Darling Jon, your face is so drawn!" she cried when she came almost to the end of hugging me. "They've been ill-treating you up in the C camp again! We will hide you here and you shall never go back to them."

"Then they will come and burn this house down and chase you and poor Anr and Pappy into the mountains!"

"Then instead we will leave altogether for some far happy country, and keep a real cow, and Pappa and you can grow figs and catch tunny in the sea."

"And you can start slimming, Bynca!"

"Pah, you're jealous because I'm a well-built girl and you're a reed."

When I introduced her to Adam, some of her smile went. She made him welcome, nonetheless, and was getting us glasses of cold tea when my father came in. Father was thin and withered and bent, and smelt as ever pleasantly of his home-grown tobacco; like my sisters, he had the settled expression of a certain kind of peasant—the kind that accepts, with protest but without malice, the vagaries of life. It is the gift life sends to compensate for the lack of a high I.Q.

"It's a long time since we saw you, son," he said to me. "I thought you'd come down before the winter came. Things don't get any better in Saint Praz, I can tell you. You know the power station broke down in Juli and they still haven't mended it—can't get the parts, Geri was telling me. We go to bed early, these cold nights, to save fuel. And you can't buy a candle these days, not for love nor money."

"Nonsense, Pappy, Anr brought us two last week from Novok market."

"Maybe, my girl, but Novok's a long way away."

When my sister Anr came in, our family was complete again—as complete as it will be on this Earth, for my mother died of a fever a dozen years ago, my elder sister Myrtyr was killed in riots when I was a child, and my two brothers walked down the valley many years since, and have never been heard of again. There's another sister, Saraj, but since she married, she has quarrelled with Pappy over a question of dowry, and the two sides are not on speaking terms.

Adam sat in our midst, sometimes sipping his tea, looking straight ahead and hardly appearing to bother to listen to our chatter. After a while, my father brought out a little leather bottle of plum brandy and dosed our coffees with some of its contents.

"Disgusting habit," he said, winking, at me, "but p'raps it'll put a bit of life into your friend, eh, Jon? You're mighty like my idea of a cerebral, Mr. Adam, too intelligent to trouble yourself with poor people like us."

"Do not become curious about me, Mr. Winther," Adam said. "I am different from other men."

"Is that a boast or a confession?" Anr asked, and she and Bynca went off into peals of laughter. I saw an old woman outside in the sunlight turn her head and smile at the sound as she went past. My cheeks flushed as I sensed the hostility between Adam and the others; it leapt into being as if a tap had been turned on.

"Adam has just come through a series of painful operations," I said, trying to apologize to both sides.

"Are you going to show us your scars, Mr. Adam?" Anr asked, still giggling.

"You don't get any fancy hospital treatment in Saint Praz if you're classified as Prole," father said. I knew that he threw it in as a general observation, as a shrewd bit of information he felt was part of his life's experience. But Adam's chip of brain would not register such undertones.

"I have become a new sort of man," he said flatly.

I saw their faces turned to him, flat and unreceptive. He did not amplify. They did not ask. Caught between them, I knew he did not think it worth while explaining anything to them; like most C's, he reciprocated the dislike of the proles. They, in their turn, suspected him of boasting—and although there were many boasters in Saint Praz, the convention was that one did it with a smile on one's face, to take away the sting, or the wrath of the devil, should he be listening.

"The curse of the human race has been animal feeling," Adam said. He was staring up at the dark rafters, his face stiff and cold, but made ludicrous for all that by his red swollen nose. "There was a time, two or three centuries ago, when it looked as if the intellect might win over the body, and our species become something worth while. But too much procreation killed that illusion."

"Are you—some sort of a better person than the rest of us?" father asked him.

"No. I am only a freak. I do not belong anywhere."

Silence would have fallen had I not said roughly, "Come off it, Adam—you're welcome here, or I wouldn't have brought you."

"And as usual you must be famished, poor things," Bynca said, jumping up. "We'll have a feast tonight, that's what! Anr, run down to old Herr Sudkinzin and see what he has left of that sow his son slaughtered on Mondai. Pappa, if you light the fire, these two convicts can have a turn in the tub tonight. I think Jon smells a bit high, like an old swine in from a muck-wallow!"

"Very like, Bynca," I said, laughing, "but if so I'm perfectly ready to be home-cured."

With a gesture that seemed halfway between reverence and contempt, my father pushed away the electric fire—useless since the power station ceased to function—from the centre of the hearth and began preparations to light the ancient iron stove. My sisters began bustling about, Anr fetching in kindling from the stack under the eaves. I stood up. They loved me here, but there was no real place for me. My real place was up in the camp, I thought—not without self-pity, but with truth; up there was my own room, shabby, yes, yet full of my books, shabby too, but duplicated right there on the camp press.

Christ's blood, that was the place my kind had chosen, over a century ago. The common people had often revolted against the rich—but the rich were not identifiable once shorn of their money; then the tide of anger turned against the intelligent. You can always tell an intellectual, even when he cowers naked and bruised before you with his spectacles squashed in the muck; you only have to get him to talk. So the intellectuals had elected to live in camps, behind wire, for their own safety. Things were better now—because we were fewer and they infinitely more; but the situation had changed again: the stay was no longer voluntary, for we had lost our place in the world. We had even lost our standing in the camps. Throughout the more-than-mediaeval darkness that had fallen over Europe, our cerebral monasteries were ruled over by the pistol and whip; and the flagellation of the new order of monks was never self-inflicted.

"Some visitors coming see you, son," father said, peering through the tiny panes of the window. He straightened his back and brushed at his coat, smiling and nodding to himself.

There was no time for thinking from then on. As Anr went down through the town to see the butcher, she called out to her friends that I was home and had brought along a strange man. Gradually those friends straggled round, to look in and drink my health in some of my father's small store of wine, and cast many a curious look at Adam, and ask me many a question about what happened in the camp —was it true that we were going to invent a sort of ray that would keep the frost from the tender spring crops, and so on.

When I was tired of talking to them, and that moment came soon, they talked amiably to each other, exchanging the gossip of Saint Praz, drinking the wine. The butcher came back with Anr, his son beside him carrying half a side of pig, and disappeared into the kitchen to help my sisters cook it. The son pushed himself a place beside our stove, and faced up to the wine with gusto. In time, my sisters, very red of cheek, returned to the room, thick by now with smoke and rumour, bearing with them a big steaming goulash, which the company devoured, laughing and splashing as they did so. We ate it with chunks of bread and followed it with black coffee. Afterwards, the visitors wished to stay and see Adam and me in the tub; but, with lewd jokes and roars of mirth, Anr and my father finally saw them off. We could hear them laughing and singing as they made their way down the street.

"You should come home more often, my boy," father said, mopping his brow as he laced the latch on the last of his guests.

"So I would father, if your neighbours didn't descend on you and eat you out of house and home every time I put in an appearance."

"Spoken like a damned cerebral," he said. "Always the thought for the morrow! No offence to you, son, but there'd be no joy in the world at all if your sort ruled. . . . Life's bad enough as it is. . . . Eh, wish your mother were alive this night, Jon. The good wine makes me feel young and randy again."

He staggered round the room while my sisters brought in the great tub in which the family's infrequent baths had been taken since the day—some years back now—when the reservoir up in the hills was ruptured by earth tremors, and the taps in the bathroom ceased to yield anything but rust.

"Where's your fragile friend Adam?" Anr asked.

For the first time, I noticed Adam was not there. His presence had been so withdrawn that his absence had left no gap. Tired though I was, I ran upstairs calling him, hurried into the yard at the back and called him there. Adam did not appear.

"Eh, leave him—he must have cleared off with the folks," father said. "Let him stay away. We shall hardly miss him."

"He's not fit to wander around alone," I said. "I must go and find him."

"I'll come with you," Bynca said, slipping into an old fur wrap that had belonged to my mother. Anr called derisively that we were wasting our time, but Bynca could see how worried I was, seized my arm, and hustled out of the door with me.

"What's so important about this man? Can't he look after himself like any other young chap?" she asked.

I tried to answer, but the cold had momentarily taken my breath away. The stars froze in the sky overhead; Jupiter steered over the shoulder of the mountain behind us, and beneath our feet the cobbles sparkled and rang. The cold immediately set up a strongpost of frost in my chest, which I tried to dislodge by coughing.

At last I said to her, "He's important—had a brain operation. Could be the beginning of a pure brain kind of man who would overturn the regime—could be a mindless kind that would give the regime a race of slaves. Naturally, both regime and the C's are interested in finding out which he is."

"I wonder they let him come out if he's so important."

"You know them, Bynca—they're keeping watch. They want to see how he behaves when he is free. So do I."

The sound of the river, tumbling in its broken bed, accompanied us down the street. I thought I could also hear voices, although the street was deserted. As we rounded the bulk of the church, the voices came clear, and we saw the knot of people standing on the bridge.

Perhaps a dozen people clustered there, most of them lately the guests of my father's house. Two of them carried lanterns, one a splendid pitch torch, which the owner held aloft. This beacon, smoking and flickering, gave the scene most of what light it had. So unexpected was the sight of them gathered there, that instinctively Bynca and I stopped dead in the middle of the road.

"Sweet Saviour!" Bynca exclaimed. I saw as she spoke what made her exclaim. Of the crowd that now partly turned to face us—was it imagination or a primitive visceral sense that instantly read their hostility?—only one figure was indifferent to our arrival. That figure was apart from the rest. It stood with its back partly turned to Bynca and me and, with its arms extended sideways at shoulder level in an attempt at balance, was trying to walk the narrow parapet that bounded the north side of the bridge.

So alarmed was I that anyone should undertake so foolish a feat, that I did not realize for a moment that it was Adam X, even though I saw the yellow C on his back. The bridge over the Quviv has stood there for many centuries, and has probably not been repaired properly since the days of the Dual Monarchy, a couple of centuries ago at least. The chest-high walls that guard either side of it are crumbled and notched by the elements and the urchins who for generations have used the bridge as their playground. But it takes a bold urchin, even bare-foot and on a bright morning, to jump up on to the top of the wall and ignore the drop on to the rocks below. And now Adam, subject to giddiness, was walking along the wall by the fitful light of a torch.

As I ran forward, I shouted, "Who put him up to doing that? Get him down at once. That man is ill!"

A hand was planted sharply in the middle of my chest. I came face to face with the butcher's son, Yari Sudkinzin. I'd watched him earlier, when he was sitting against our stove, contriving to get more than his fair share of the wine.

"Keep out of this, you C!" he said. "Your buddy friend here is just showing us what he can do."

"If you made him get up there, get him down at once. He'll slip to his death at any minute."

"He insisted on doing it, get it? Said he would show us he was as good as us. You'd better stand back if you know what's good for you."

And as he was speaking, the women with him clustered about us, telling him earnestly, "We told him he was mad, but he would do it, he would do it, he would climb up there!"

Breaking through them, I went to Adam, carefully now, so that I would not startle him. His broken shoes rasped against the crumbled stone at the level of my chest. He moved very slowly, one small step at a time. He would be frozen before he got across, if he got across. He was coming now to the first of the little bays that hung out from the bridge and housed benches for the convenience of pedestrians. The angles he would have to turn would make his task more dangerous. Below us, the Quviv roared and splashed without cease.

"Come down, Adam," I said, "It's Jon Winther here. Let me help you down!"

He said only one thing to me, but it explained much that had led to his climbing up where he was: "I will show them what a superman can do."

"Adam—it's time we were tucked in a warm bed by the side of the fire. Give me your hand."

For answer, he kicked out sideways at me.

His shoe caught me a light knock on the cheek. He lost his footing entirely, and was falling even as he struck me. I grabbed at his foot, at his trousers, cried aloud, felt myself dragged sharply against the parapet, my elbows rasped over it, as his weight came into my grasp, and his body disappeared over the wall.

He made no sound!

For a ghastly moment I thought I too was going to be carried below with him. The roar of the Quviv over its rocks sounded horribly loud. Without thought, I let go of him—perhaps because of fear, perhaps because of the pain in my arms, or the cold in my body, or perhaps because of some deeper, destructive thing that emerged in me for a second. I let go of him, and he would have fallen to his death had not two of the men in the party managed to grasp him almost as I let go.

Panting and cursing, they pulled Adam up over the wall, and dumped him like a sack of potatoes on to the bench. His nose was bleeding, otherwise he seemed unharmed. But he did not speak.

"That's all your doing!" young Yari Sudkinzin said to me. "He was nearly a dead 'un, thanks to you!"

"I could draw a moral far less comforting for you," I told him. "Why don't you clear off home?"

In the end they did go, leaving Bynca and me to return with Adam's two rescuers, who supported Adam up the street. In the way that news travels in our towns, several people were already lighting up their lamps and peering from their windows and doors to see what was going on; along the road, I heard the militia questioning—I hoped—the butcher's son. With this prompting, we made what haste we could, home.

Father and Anr made a great bother when we got back. I went to lie down and warm myself by the fire, while all the aspects of what had happened were thrashed out with Bynca. After a while, Adam, who had bathed his face in a bucket outside, came and slumped down beside me, stretching as I did on the reed mats before the stove.

"There is less irrationality up in the camp," he said. "Let us go back. At least we understand that they hit us because they hate us."

"You must tell me, Adam—Grabowicz will want to know—why you did that foolish thing on the bridge. To accept a stupid dare like that is the work of a child, but to show such a lack of fear is inhuman. What are you, how do you analyse yourself?"

He made a noise that imitated a laugh. "Nobody can understand me," he said. "I can't understand myself until there are more like me."

I told him then. "I can't work on these brain operations any more."

"Grabowicz can. Grabowicz will. You're too late to be squeamish, Jon; already there is a new force in the world."

After what I had seen on the bridge, I felt he might be right. But a new force for good or bad? How would the change come? What would it be? I closed my eyes and saw clearly the sort of world that Grabowicz and I, with the unwitting co-operation of the prole leaders, might have already brought into being. Given enough men and women like Adam, with their visceral brains removed, they would bring up children unswayed and unsoftened by human emotion, whose motives were inscrutable to the rest of mankind. The rulers of our world would find such people very useful at first, and so a place would be made for them. And from being instruments of power, they would turn into a power in their own right. It was a process often witnessed by history.

I rolled over and looked at Adam. He appeared to be already asleep. Perhaps he was dreaming one of his sterile dreams, without incident, or body, or turmoil. Despairing, I too tried to close down my mind.

As I lay there with my eyes shut, my old father, thinking me asleep, stooped to kiss my forehead before settling himself to sleep on the fireside bench.

"I must go back to camp tomorrow, father," I murmured.

But in the morning—this morning—my father and my sisters prevailed on me to stay till the afternoon, to share their frugal midday meal with them and then go.

I sit now in the upstairs room where Anr and Bynca sleep, catching the first of the sun as it struggles clear of the mountain ridge, and trying to write this account. I feel that something awful is about to happen, that we are at one of those turning points in the story of the world. A secret record may be useful for those who come after.

Adam sits downstairs, silent. It is strange that one feeble man . . .

The militia are downstairs! They forced their way in, and I hear them shout for me and Adam. Of course the tale of last night got back up there. Dear Bynca will be downstairs, confronting them with her plump arms folded, giving me time to get away. But I must go back with them, to the camp. Perhaps if I killed Grabowicz . . .

This manuscript shall go under the loose floor board that we used to call "Bynca's board", when we were kids, so long ago. They'll never find it there, or get it except over her dead body.

HAGGARD HONEYMOON

by

JOSEPH GREEN AND JAMES WEBBERT

On other planets, even of an Earth-type nature, the general environment will be totally alien to that to which Mankind has been accustomed. However, it may well be that the dangers to human beings will be unseen—as the following story by two American authors points out.

HAGGARD HONEYMOON

Haggard's Meteorite: The origin of its name is lost in obscurity, but its importance to the human race will never be forgotten. First recorded on Canopus 37 on August 27, 2024 Ertime, this meteorite for a period of thirty years supplied Earth's need for uranium virtually alone. The Hundred-Year Quest for the control of hydrogen fusion, the most baffling scientific mystery of all time, ended in success just before the Haggard mine yielded its last worthwhile ore. It is interesting to speculate whether the opportune discovery of this great mine made interstellar travel possible, or if man's venture into space might have collapsed at the beginning for lack of the only fuel known at the time capable of powering the great starships.

An interesting note on the mining operation the Space Service conducted on Canopus 37 will be found in the section dealing with new maladies and diseases encountered on other worlds.

HISTORY OF GALACTIC EXPLORATION

One

He came trudging along the jungle trail in the last of the fading light, a big man, young, his shoulders drooping in fatigue. Valle, the needlebrush poised, stood watching until he reached the little garden and sank wearily into a bamboo chair. She made a final light stroke, outlining a bright leaf, and stepped back to admire the effect.

"Is this the way you greet a tired husband home after a hard day's work?" asked Carter Mason gruffly.

His bride of six weeks studied the unfinished painting a

moment more, then turned towards him, flung her arms out in dramatic appeal, and recited:

> *"If I should meet thee*
> *After long years,*
> *How should I greet thee?*
> *With silence and tears."*

He lunged forward out of the chair, caught one of the extended hands and pulled her, laughing, on to his lap as he settled down again. "It's only been since this morning, Mrs. Mason. Now kiss me and tell me what's for dinner, in that order."

"But it *seemed* like years," she said instead, struggling to sit upright. He released her quickly, always mindful not to impose his strength on hers. She found a more comfortable position on his lap and kissed him leisurely and with great thoroughness.

"How did it go today?" she asked gently when their lips parted.

"Not too bad. I picked up a chunk that weighed in at forty kilograms, and Sorenhirst found two that weighed fifty together."

"Pure uranium as usual?"

"The pure stuff. We just don't find anything else down there."

Valle wriggled off his lap and to her feet, a small, slim young woman with very dark hair and eyes and an olive complexion. "Dinner's on the table, and there's a movie at the Centre at eight. Feel up to it?"

"Of course," he agreed automatically, though he would have been perfectly content to stay home with her and go to bed early. Ten hours hard work in this planet's low-oxygen atmosphere was enough activity for one day.

The little three-room cottage sat in a small clearing out in the heart of the forest, and it was refreshingly cool inside. He flicked a switch as they stepped indoors and the orange glare of the insect-repelling lights came on in the garden. Electricity was the only luxury these cottages afforded, and since they were of slat and bamboo construction the bugs would have eaten a sleeper alive if not kept away. Canopus 37, or McKeever as it was more popularly known, was a tropical world, with a climate similar to that of Earth's equatorial zone across three-quarters of its surface, and the temperature did not change more than ten degrees the year round.

Their assigned *Rilli* servant, whom they called Jake, stood waiting at the head of the small rough table, wearing his usual blank expression. The natives of McKeever were humanoids less than a meter high, with very broad shoulders and sturdy bodies covered with a thin coat of brown or black fur. Their earless heads were round as balls and apparently made of solid bone, to judge by their percipience. When the McKeever project first started an effort had been made to train them for work in the mine, but it had been abandoned after a few months. The *Rilli* seemed constantly lost in a dream world of their own, and the intelligence, which was one of their manifest characteristics when they chose to display it, was seldom used.

Their dinner consisted of the fruits and nuts which grew locally in great profusion, supplemented by one meat dish from the kitchen in the Centre. Carter ate with the intentness of a man who must consume vast quantities of fuel for conversion into energy. Valle dawdled with her food, but ate a fair meal.

He took a shower after eating, room-temperature water drained from an overhead wooden barrel, and when he was dressed again Jake had finished his work and gone and Valle had slipped into a dress and was waiting. He dropped a sonic insect repellant in his pocket and they headed for the Centre.

McKeever received little starlight but had three very bright moons, of which at least two were always in the night sky. The *Rilli* kept the paths from the cottages to the Centre free of new growth and McKeever's numerous carnivores were too small to be dangerous to humans. It was a peaceful half-kilometre to the Centre and they strolled leisurely along, arms about each other, two honeymooners lost in each other and the charm of the night.

Carter Mason stared downward at the bright young face turned up to the moonlight, felt the movement of the pliant waist under his arm, and wondered how long this could last, and where the catch was hidden.

The big blond man with the crewcut searched his memory as they walked, and just before they emerged into the open area where the Centre stood recalled a favourite remnant. In a hushed voice he quoted:

"She walks in beauty, like the night
Of cloudless climes and starry skies;
And all that's best of dark and bright
Meet in her aspect and her eyes."

Valle laughed, delighted. "I thought I was the nineteenth century poet fiend. You quote Byron like a professor."

"The only thing I ever memorized," he said, grinning, and then they were in the open and saying hello to other couples converging on the brightly lit Centre.

There were twenty-one couples present, one-half the human population of the planet, and every person there was between twenty-five and thirty years of age, each couple had been married the day before they left Earth, and no person had been there longer than five and a half Ermonths. In two weeks the bi-monthly ship from Earth would fall into orbit over the base and the fire-belching chemical-powered shuttles would bring down fourteen more couples, and take away fourteen families and some five thousand kilograms of pure uranium, of which roughly one thousand would be used on the return trip. The McKeever Operation paid a little over two to one on uranium production, and the factor which kept the average so low was the weight of twenty-eight human bodies, and the support systems to keep them alive, which had to ride both ways each trip. No person stayed on McKeever more than six Ermonths.

They found seats on the rough wooden benches the *Rilli* had made for the main recreation room and settled down to enjoy the film. Two old-timers, Adam and Joy Parkinson, who would be leaving on the next ship, were sitting on their right. Carter noticed before the lights dimmed that Adam was leaning forward, tensed, and Joy was watching him with a troubled expression on her sharp young face.

The film was a dramatic love story, one some deskbound bureaucrat on Earth felt proper for a group of young honeymooners isolated on a foreign planet. The plotline had two newlyweds kidnapped by a psychopath who hated women, and built steadily towards a very dramatic finish. At the climax, when the psychopath was approaching the terrified girl with a flashing knife, while the young husband lay bound and helpless, Carter felt Adam stirring by his side, and suddenly the nervous man bounded to his feet and screamed, the sound a harsh and jarring reality which shattered the illusion created by the screen. The lights came on instantly, and Adam stood looking wildly around at the small audience, his face still white with terror. Then he put his hands to his face and sank shuddering back into his seat. Joy stood leaning over him comfortingly, her thin face concerned.

Colonel Simpson, the ranking officer and a three-month man, came swiftly from the projection room, where his pretty wife had been serving as operator, and motioned Carter out of his seat. The little group stood milling uncertainly for a moment as Simpson sat down and talked with Adam and Joy, then slowly began to drift out of the door, all interest in the movie forgotten. Colonel Simpson's voice stopped them.

"Your attention, please, everyone. Adam Parkinson is reporting to the hospital immediately, and Joy is appointed as his nurse. He will be relieved of active duty until the ship arrives. The rest of you please report for work as usual in the morning."

There was an excited buzz of speculation as the group broke up into small knots, but Carter ignored it and led Valle swiftly away. He had heard enough of Simpson's conversation with the Parkinsons to get the general drift. And he thought he saw the catch to a Haggard Honeymoon.

Valle asked no questions until they were on their private path, but then they tumbled out in a confused heap. Carter hushed her gently with a big palm and slowed his rapid pace. McKeever's air had an oxygen content of only sixteen per cent, and even after one learned deep-breathing techniques it did not pay to over-exert yourself.

"Simpson was asking Adam how he'd been sleeping lately, and if he had nightmares," the big man said slowly. "The answer was that he hardly slept at all, and if he did his dreams were so bad they almost drove him crazy. Joy confirmed that Adam hadn't rested well for a month, and that he'd been having nightmares from which he'd wake up in the middle of the night, screaming. This is the first time it happened while he was awake, and I heard Simpson say something about that being the final sign."

"Final sign? Sign of what?"

"The reason no one stays here longer than six months, obviously. Apparently men on McKeever are peculiarly susceptible to mental derangement, and after six months they start cracking up. At least that's the gist of what he told Joy and Adam. He also said it seldom affected women, and that Adam would be all right once he got away from here."

"Mental derangement? I thought this tour was limited to six months because of the thin air, the hard work, and so on. Where does mental illness come in?"

"We were all led to believe that, but no one ever actually said it aloud. And no one explained why they only accepted engaged couples for this assignment, or why they go to such pains to give you ideal honeymoon conditions. And especially, no one explained why students straight out of college started with a captain's commission in the Space Service."

"Do you suppose this all ties in together? If so, why hasn't someone explained it, and why are you sent out here unprepared?"

"I don't know, but tomorrow I'm going to try to find out."

When he reported to the Centre next morning Simpson was waiting for him. "Carter, you're going to take Major Parkinson's place in administration, starting tomorrow. Come by here on your way home for a briefing."

He climbed on the little runabout that was the base's only powered land vehicle in numbed surprise. The base organization structure was very simple. There was a colonel for a C.O., three majors, and the rest captains. Every man on the base except the C.O. worked, one of the majors in charge of each shift at the mine and the third in administration, which consisted primarily of overseeing the maintenance work performed by the *Rilli* and the kitchen-work done by the wives.

The other young captains on the day shift pounded him heartily on the back and congratulated him as they rolled to the mine. Major Parkinson had what was considered the best job on the base. He did no physical work, and was in constant contact with all the pretty young wives. Carter took their good-natured kidding with a grin, but was glad when they reached the Changehouse and he could hop out and get into his suit.

The Changehouse was a big building, of locally mixed concrete, sitting on the edge of the small round lake that was Haggard's mine. The walls were radiation-proof through sheer massiveness. One large room was open to the lake, and from here a wide ramp led downward at a sharp angle into the red water. The three crawlers, small submersible radiation-proof tanks with front-mounted shovels and an open cargo compartment at the rear, stood at the water's edge where the night shift had left them.

In the outer room Carter and the rest of the day crew stripped to the buff and donned soft, protective underwear, then the heavy, awkward suit. It was made of eight layers of alternating silk and lead foil, with a small airtank strapped to the back and a polarized vision-glass three inches thick.

Carter and his partner, Buckley, stepped through the door marked DANGER : RADIATION and walked over to their crawler. They made the usual exterior inspection and then climbed inside. Buckley took the operator's chair and activated the control board. He checked his indicators carefully, then turned on the pump and eased the power control forward. The crawlers were powered by a small reactor cooled by Nak, a sodium-potassium solution which circulated through an outer jacket over the reactor and passed through a heat-exchanger on the opposite end of its cycle. The heat-exchanger generated steam, which was in turn used to drive a turbine. The turbine turned a D.C. generator which supplied usable power. It was the simplest system anyone had been able to devise where uranium was the only fuel available, but woefully inefficient compared to the giant atom-smashers which powered the starships.

When the turbine reached operating speed Buckley fed

current to the high-torque motors turning the tracks and the crawler eased forward. They trundled to the ramp leading into the reddish water and felt the familiar lurch as it eased over the edge and started downward. Buckley turned on the outside lights as the water rose in a red veil around them.

Two

THE crater Haggard's Meteorite had created when it struck McKeever some thousand Eryears back was a half-kilometre wide and sixty metres deep, circular in outline and filled with the only red water known on the planet. The bottom was covered with the accumulated silt of years, level in some areas, but heaped in odd shapes and forms in others. The crawlers were slowly and methodically removing the entire lake bottom to the Changehouse, where it was sifted for uranium and returned to a far portion of the lake in the form of mud. So far the yield had been incredibly high, so much so that this one mine was supplying the entire Space Service fleet.

Buckley followed the tracks of the night shift across the silt to their work area, a reddish mound near the centre where the yield had been good, and manoeuvred the crawler into position. Carter, acting as co-pilot for the moment, watched the dials on the control board. Buckley moved them forward at full speed and when the grinding tracks had the shovel buried deep in the muck he lifted sharply upward. The crawler started to lurch forward as the shovel came free, but Buckley eased up on the power and threw it into reverse. As the machine moved backward the shovel continued to rise, describing a full half-circle and dumping its contents in the cargo compartment at the rear. Then forward again for another scoop, rocking and jouncing on the uneven lake-bottom.

When the compartment would hold no more Buckley retained the last scoop in the shovel and headed for the ramp. They broke water in a moment and continued up the ramp to the dumping chute. A ton of red water, mud, silt, filth—and maybe an ingot of uranium—went tumbling into the gaping maw. Inside the Changehouse other men, working with hands shielded from deadly radiation only by the thickness of their gloves, sorted the solid particles out of the mess and washed them clean. These were taken to a small spectroscope and carefully checked, while the effluvia of mud and slime was washed into the long, open sluice that sloped gently downward out of the massive building and ended in a far corner of the lake.

The large pump which made it possible for the Changehouse to operate, the atomic-powered generator which supplied the small settlement with electrical power, and the three crawlers and the little runabout were the only heavy items of Earth manufacture on McKeever. The Centre, their cottages, and their food were all supplied by the planet itself. Every kilogram saved on weight was a kilogram reserved for uranium. The Service even preferred small men, when they could get ones who met their unusual and exacting standards. Big men like Carter Mason were rare on McKeever.

At noon they took a short break to eat, and then changed places and continued the long grind. And finally the day ended, the night shift reported in, and they were free to go. McKeever had a twenty-two Erhour rotation and the men worked two ten-hour shifts. During the two hours slack time each morning, repairs were made to the equipment, the sluice was cleaned and the safety equipment carefully and competently checked. Each man caught two hours slack time each week. They had arbitrarily assigned a seven-day week to the planet, since the seasons changed the weather very little, and worked six of those seven days.

Carter was dog-tired, as usual, when he hopped off the runabout and reported to Colonel Simpson in the small room he called his office. Billie, Simpson's pretty wife, who acted as the commander's secretary, motioned him to a seat.

"Any luck today?"

"Not much. A few bits and pieces."

"That's too bad. Rest a moment and I'll get Bert. I think he's in the kitchen."

She was gone less than two minutes and returned with her husband, animatedly discussing as they walked some aspect of managing the kitchen force of eight wives. As a wife Billie had no official status, but unofficially she managed the women's work force under the supervision of the major in administration.

There were lines of strain on Simpson's face when he sat down and hitched forward in his chair, to rest his elbows on the desk and his face in his hands. There was silence for a moment, and then Simpson asked, "Tell me, Mason, have you ever wondered why we have a somewhat un-military set-up here?"

"I expect we all have, sir. But the hours are so long and you're kept so busy; and being new-marrieds . . ." he let the statement go unfinished. The absorption of each new couple in the joys of sex, and the manifold aspects of marriage under such strange but satisfying conditions, easily accounted for time-consumption.

"Let me give you some background that was left out of your orientation courses, Mason. First, the Space Service tried for two years to mine Haggard's Meteorite, with little success. The attempt was almost abandoned, and would have been except for one of those freaks of chance that happen now and then, even in the Space Service. A young lieutenant, fresh out of the Academy and just married, was assigned to McKeever. Service wasn't voluntary then. He tried to get out of it and it was impossible. Rumours had been getting around of what it was like here and the young wife knew her chances of getting back a sane husband were only one-in-three. She pulled off the virtually impossible stunt of stowing away on a military ship and went with her husband. Once here, of course, there was little they could do. Every gramme of return weight was needed for uranium. So she stayed, and the base commander built the first of the honeymoon cottages."

Simpson studied his fingers a moment, then continued, "There was no set period of duty then. A man stayed until he showed signs of cracking up, and was shipped home on the next ship. The average man lasted two months, some as long as four. It took two out of every three grammes mined just to haul the crews back and forth! The young lieutenant made the usual two months with no problems, then four, and then eight. During his tenth month he showed signs of cracking and both he and his wife were returned, with a full pardon for her violation of military rules. On the next shipment two couples were sent, to see if it was a freak chance or a breakthrough. One couple had been married eight years and were still childless, the second another pair of honeymooners. The older married man lasted four months, the younger eight. That was enough for the high brass. From then on all McKeever recruits were young, new-married, and highly compatible couples. And for the first time the system started showing a real profit."

"A first-class case of empirical reasoning, eh? And it worked. But tell me, why was no effort made to find the conditions that caused the derangement and eliminate them?"

Simpson smiled briefly. "Efforts were made and the trouble was located. But doing something about it turned out to be a different matter. It seems that the atmosphere around the lake is loaded with very high-frequency energy waves of unknown origin, so faint it takes our best instruments to detect them at all. It's like nothing we've ever experienced, and frankly, the best scientists we could get up here were completely lost. In the end it was decided we'd work our way around them, not through them, after this honeymoon method was discovered. No one quite knows why, but the effect is pronouncedly less apparent on young people who have an overpowering interest in life besides themselves. Also, women are apparently immune or the effect is so mild no one has stayed long enough to be hurt. That first lieutenant's wife stayed ten months with no ill effects, and no woman since has been affected in her six months stay."

"Has anyone failed to recover after being returned to Earth?"

Simpson turned away and stared at the blank wall of his office. "A few. Some of them are still in asylums on Earth."

For the first time bitterness crept into Mason's voice. "And we weren't told this. We were told about the captain's commission, the hard work and long hours, the ideal honeymoon conditions, and the unusual fact our wives could accompany us for duty tours on a foreign planet. Nothing more!"

"There is a very good reason for this, which is why you will tell no one else, including your wife. You last longer if you stay ignorant. Brooding brings it on. Only yourself and the two other majors know the full story. Not even Billie is in on it. And it's quite possible Parkinson could have made his six months without trouble if he hadn't known."

"I'm afraid it's a little late for that. Valle and I were discussing Parkinson's behaviour on the way home from the movie. We came quite close to guessing the answer."

"Then don't discuss it any further, and ask Valle not to let the word get around to the other wives. This is quite important."

"I'll do my best, sir," said Mason, rising. It was apparent from Simpson's manner that the interview was at an end.

Carter Mason went home to the loving arms of his wife, and next morning reported to his new duties as administrative officer. He swiftly discovered, with the help of Billie Simpson, that Parkinson had been holding down a complex job entailing endless record-keeping and some rather exacting personal relationship problems. One of his primary responsibilities had been the keeping of the peace between eighty-four young people of many and varied backgrounds who were unexpectedly thrown into close proximity under very unusual conditions. The expected cause of trouble, infidelity, was relatively rare, although light flirtations were a common and recurring event. Still, there were many causes of conflict inherent in the situation itself, and Parkinson's prime job seemed to have been to keep them at a minimum. It did not take Carter long to decide he had been picked for promotion as much for his degree in psychology as his native abilities.

When the shuttle took Parkinson away two weeks later he had to be carried aboard. He was not violent, but he seemed to have lost the faculty of self-control. Joy, her thin face white with grief, was by his side. Simpson watched them go without changing expression, and when the little ship cleared ground he turned to Carter and said, "According to the best information I have he's only in the beginning stages. He should recover almost fully before he reaches Earth. The only ones in whom it didn't clear up were those already in the violent stage."

Carter shuddered slightly, and returned to his duties. The ship had brought a batch of paper for his attention.

It was a month later when he awoke from a deep sleep to a sound of low sobbing, and discovered his wife was shivering violently in the narrow bed, and crying in her sleep.

He sat up in bed and pulled her into his arms, comforting her tenderly and bringing her gradually from sleep to wakefulness. After a time the shivering eased and she grew quieter. He continued to pet and hold her until she finally pushed away and sat up in the bed, her nude body a dim but lovely presence in the deep shadows. "I'm . . . all right, darling. It's faded away now. But what a terrible nightmare; I was flying, and had wings, but I didn't beat them, I just flew, and——"

"Easy now, don't try to recall the dream, it will only disturb you again," he soothed her. "Lie down and try to get back to sleep. It's late."

"I don't know if I ever want to sleep again," she said simply. "That horrible . . . *thing*! . . . that attacked me while I was flying. It had huge claws, and locked them in my back and started tearing at my neck with its great beak. . . . I was falling. . . ." She sobbed again, and then the tears came, full of a deep but unexplainable grief, and she cuddled into his arms and let them flow. From there she passed into a light doze, one unmarked by any sign of dreaming, and he eased her back to the bed and pulled the light sheet over themselves again. He held her close to his own body while she passed into deep slumber, and gradually dozed off again himself.

She was her usual buoyant self in the morning as she prepared his breakfast, and he could almost have thought the incident forgotten if there had not been unusual dark shadows around her large eyes.

Carter pondered Valle's odd description of the dream during the short walk to work. That "feeling of falling" was an old and easily explained dream symbol, but the odd description of flying without using wings and the other attacking birds—those were out of no textbook he had ever read. It aroused an immediate and pressing question. Was this a natural dream, brought on by some factor as simple as indigestion, or a manifestation of the derangement that plagued the inhabitants of McKeever?

His question was answered the next night, when Valle dreamed again, and this time it was something so unworldly, so completely out of keeping with her background that it almost had to be caused by an outside source. It was no worse than the night before, but two in a row was too much for him to tackle alone. He took the matter up with Simpson as soon as he got to work.

The commanding officer held his head in his hands and stared at his home-made desk top, his face a study in misery. When he raised his gaze his face was sober and cold. "What would you say if I told you I had almost exactly the same dream you described the same night?"

"I'd say that since you're almost a five-month man it might reasonably be expected. I'd also say I don't see what that has to do with the problem. According to these records I've inherited it's normal, almost expected, for a man to start getting the bad dreams in his fifth month. It's never happened to a woman before."

"True, and it is a complicating factor. But if you'll check you'll probably find that half the five-month men here had the same dreams as myself and Valle on the same nights. Don't you find this significant?"

"Not particularly. We already know it's caused by microwave energy forms of some description. It's not too odd that it should have a roughly similar effect on human beings, enough to at least give you similar dreams."

"No two human beings are that similar, Carter. Assuming that the force acts identically on any two humans, why should it inspire almost identical dreams? Valle and I, for instance, have completely different backgrounds, come from different world states, are of different nationality. The odds against a given stimulus causing us to dream the same dream are astronomical, yet we not only did but so did every other affected man on this planet. No, there has to be a logical explanation, and so far we haven't found it."

"I've got a more pressing problem. Valle and I need to go back on the next ship, not wait the extra two months for our regular turn. According to all records breakdown comes within a few weeks of the commencement of the dreaming."

Simpson sighed. "I know. And it means not only a loss of shipping weight next time but a disruption of our organization here. We'll be shy a couple for two months. But I'm afraid it can't be helped. Go ahead and cut orders for yourselves. I'll sign them."

Three

It was two nights later when he came up out of a heavy sleep to find Valle shaking him. "Carter, wake up! You sleep like a dead man! Carter, listen, I think I've discovered something tonight. The dream was beautiful for a change, something about lovely colours floating across the sky, with hordes of little *Rilli* chasing after them. But tonight, for the first time, I could tell that something was pushing those dreams at me, making me go through them whether I wanted to or not. And Carter . . . whatever it was was a living intelligence!"

Jarred fully awake, he sat up and turned on the room's single lamp. Valle, who was not very modest, made no pretence of covering herself, but leaned forward earnestly and said, "I could feel direction and control behind those dreams. It was like being an actor in a play, but instead of knowing your lines and reciting them you really *lived* the part, and felt and touched and tasted everything the actor did. But it was all so weird and three-quarters of it wasn't understandable in human terms. I kept trying to make sense out of it, and when I did I seemed to get lost. . . ."

Her voice trailed away, then resumed, "And my head started hurting, and I woke up. I don't think it would have been so bad if I hadn't insisted on trying to understand the dream."

There was no intelligent life whatever on McKeever, with the possible exception of the *Rilli*, and they were in a doubtful category. Or could it be that there was an intelligent lifeform not yet discovered? Possibly creatures so small they had so far escaped observation, and used this weird method of making their presence felt?

There was no way they could resolve the puzzle that night, and they gave it up and went to sleep. Next morning Carter told Simpson of Valle's feelings, and found that it was not a new discovery. "Several other people have reported the same impressions. But we've never been able to prove it one way or the other. And usually," he hesitated, then continued, "when an affected man gets to that stage—he's pretty far gone."

"But Valle had her first dream only three nights back! You said it usually takes several weeks from the first signs."

"Yes, and I was talking about men. She's the first woman ever to be affected. I don't know where the difference lies, but I can tell you I don't like it."

They left it on that unsatisfactory note, and Carter took a fast hike to the Changehouse to pick up the weekly report. Major Chen Yi, in charge of the day shift this week, had it ready, and Carter paused for a moment's conversation before heading back. "How's the pickings this week?"

Chen Yi, a small, dapper man with a drive far larger than his size, who had majored in celestial navigation in college, picked his teeth with a splinter and spat in the dirt. They were standing just outside the closed entrance to the main flushing room, as close as Carter could go unless he wanted to put on a protective suit. "About as usual. We'll have all the ship can carry next month."

Carter thought of telling him they would be shipping two hundred kilograms less than usual this trip, but restrained himself. There was no point in letting word of Valle's troubles leak out any sooner than it must.

Carter turned and stared out over the placid surface of the red lake, pondering, as he had a thousand times before, the many enigmas hidden in that sultry water. A lake whose bottom was covered with odd, huge formations, where pure uranium was lying about in profusion, whose water contained an element that defied analysis but which was the best radioactive shield known, so good an inch of it over a piece of uranium enabled you to wet your finger over it and not get burned. A lake that contained water found nowhere else on the planet, a lake that, by itself, was supplying all the uranium needed for Earth's far-ranging interstellar fleet.

"That must have been quite a blow when this junior-sized planetoid came whistling down through the atmosphere and smashed into this planet," said Carter softly. "A wonder it didn't drive McKeever out of its orbit."

Chen Yi turned and stared at him, his slanted eyes twinkling. "It wasn't too bad an impact. It hit at a relatively slow speed, just a few hundred kilometres an hour, and it didn't have the mass you seem to think. It was hollow."

It was Carter's turn to stare. "Hollow? You're kidding me. And how could you know?"

"The distribution of the fragments and the shape of the lake. And a little elementary maths will prove the speed point. It came straight down and dug in without bouncing, creating a roughly round lake. The material was semi-metallic, as you know. The soil here is only a few metres thick, and the soft limestone under it extends well below the depth of the lake. For practical purposes you can forget the soil. Just figure on a round metallic object hitting the limestone and digging down. You'll get so many metres of penetration per so many metres per second of speed. Be glad to show you the math sometime."

"No, thanks, it would probably be over my head anyway. But tell me, where did you come up with idea of a hollow meteorite?"

The smaller man smiled briefly. "Already had the idea. Just wanted some proof of it, theoretical if nothing better. Hasn't it occurred to you, Carter, that it is impossible to explain this," he swept a hand at the red lake, "in terms of natural phenomena?"

Carter had to smile. He wasn't the only one for whom honeymoon conditions were not a sufficient antidote to thought. "You tell me."

"All right, I'll spell it out. The object which hit here was a ship, not a meteorite. It was almost a half-kilometre in diameter and spherical in shape. It was composed of a semi-metallic alloy with which we are completely unfamiliar, and used a damping agent for its nuclear drive which was soluble in water, and turned it red. And it wasn't from this galaxy." Chen Yi turned and stared into the north-west sky, where the bright sun hid the stars from view. "Our nearest neighbours the Magellanic Clouds," he pointed with a small finger. "Large or small, take your pick. Earth's supply of uranium came from one of them."

Carter walked back to the Administration building in a thoughtful, almost dazed, silence.

Just before he entered the door he paused and stared a moment at the only building, other than those of the base, on the planet McKeever. Just the tip of the tower could be seen in the distance, and in a way it was as great a marvel as Haggard's Meteorite. The *Rilli* had felled some of the largest trees in the vicinity, giants towering over sixty metres high, and, by engineering methods forgotten or ignored in the present day, hauled them to the crest of the only hill in the vicinity. There they erected a high tower to their unknown god. The area round the tower was strictly taboo to all Earthmen and most of the *Rilli,* only the tribal leaders, priests, and guards having access to the grounds. The top of the tower was the holy-of-holies to the little people. Other than that abortive attempt to use them as miners the *Rilli* had not received much attention from the busy Earthmen, and they deserved more study.

Carter finished the day's work in thoughtful silence and wound his weary way homeward, arm in arm with Valle, whose turn it had been in the kitchens. It seemed odd that so much could be known about McKeever, and yet so little understood. This malady that struck Earth people so mercilessly, so senselessly, which was so well defined and so meagrely comprehended—where did it originate? Was it a natural phenomenon produced in some strange way by the planet's magnetic field? Could there be any meaning to the puzzling fact that the afflicted persons seemed to feel, in the latter stages, that the dreams they experienced were directed at them by an intelligent entity? Or was this only a sign of incipient breakdown, the standard paranoid delusion of persecution? And most important of all . . . Valle. There was almost a month to endure before the next shuttle, and if the case histories he had examined were any indication she was going off the deep end at a rate approximately four times the previous record. Two more days would find her mind trembling dangerously close to the brink of accepting the unreal, another week might render her insane beyond recovery. She could not possibly stay a full month unless her dangerous progress downhill was somehow arrested.

And there was no possible way in which she could be removed from McKeever.

Valle had another dream that night, worse than the last, and woke up screaming. She stayed awake the rest of the night and he made some coffee and stayed up with her.

Something had to be done, and after talking it over with Colonel Simpson he tried the only antidote that seemed a possibility. He gave Valle a strong sedative the next night, and sat with her until she drifted off to a drugged sleep. He could tell from her deep, slow breathing that she was at least two levels below normal unconsciousness, and decided to get some rest himself, but first he set the alarm for an hour earlier than usual, though he badly needed the rest. He did not intend for Valle's drugged slumber to fade into normal sleep on the road to wakefulness.

He experienced the first dream himself that night, but it was so faint it bothered him very little. Well before dawn he was up and checking on Valle, who was beginning to twitch slightly but still seemed unusually deep in sleep. He made coffee and carried it to her bedside, then brought her rapidly up out of sleep into full wakefulness, immediately forcing her to take an oral stimulant followed by coffee. She smiled gratefully through the mental fog as she sipped the coffee and tried to throw off the effects of the sedative. When she could talk intelligibly she said, "It worked, darling. No dreams."

"One. I had it," he answered briefly, then smiled at her instant apprehension. "No problem. Very minor affair which shouldn't bother me too much before we leave. It's you I'm worried about."

"This is going to be an awful way to sleep, but we'll manage," she said, and summoned a wan smile. He could not force himself to smile back.

He saw her at noon, when she came into Administration on an errand, and she looked perfectly happy. But he was still ten steps from their door that night when he heard her terrified scream.

He made those ten steps in two jumps and burst inside

to find her facing a puzzled and apprehensive Jake, still screaming, her small mouth an ugly rictus of terror.

He reached her and swept her into his arms, where she collapsed, sobbing in relief. Jake, his round face alternating between fright, stupidity, and puzzlement, stood in indecision for a moment, then observed that the tall ones were paying no attention to him and hastily left. He had known many men behave oddly after being on McKeever for a time, but this slim and dark-eyed tall one was the first woman he had seen go to pieces this way. But then, the ways of the tall ones were usually incomprehensible to him anyway. All he could be certain of was that they furnished the best knives, axes, cooking pots, and arrowheads his people had ever seen, and gave them away for ridiculously low numbers of hours of labour.

Behind him in the little honeymoon cottage Mason comforted the sobbing Valle as best he could, and got the story from her. "It—it was horrible, Carter! I was—was fixing your dinner, not thinking about the dreams at all, and was feeling so happy because you'd soon be home, and—suddenly the kitchen around me just seemed to fade away, as though it were made of smoke, and I was out between the stars, riding on a great bird, and a voice was reciting what seemed to be poetry, but in a tongue I couldn't understand, and lights appeared ahead of me, and a great wind started to blow, the lights got closer and it grew cold, so cold I knew I'd soon die, and *the lights*! *The lights!*"

She collapsed into sobbing again, but soon recovered and continued: "When the lights drew near I could see they were gigantic light-emitting eyes, eyes on creatures like none I've seen in my worst dreams, and riding on these creatures were man-like things I could tell were *Rilli*, but not like Jake and these others, huge things taller than you are but wide like the *Rilli*, and their eyes flashed and they had great swords they whirled over their heads, and they shouted as they charged me. And I could tell that there were hundreds of others just like me out there between the stars, riding those huge birds, and we had come to fight these giant men. And—and one of them came at me, swinging that great sword.

"His eyes were flashing like stars themselves, his mouth was open and he was roaring some war-song, that great sword came flying for my throat and I tried to dodge, to turn, and then—it seems odd to tell it, but I'd been trying all along to wake up, to get away from that scene because in another part of my mind I knew it was all illusion, it *had* to be illusion, and I wanted so desperately to wake up, I was trying all the time to force my eyes to see something besides the blackness and the stars, and when I saw that sword coming at me I closed my eyes and screamed. I actually felt the sword cut into my neck and knew I was dead in another thousandth of a second if I didn't pull away and I tried and opened my eyes again and there was Jake in front of me, staring at me pop-eyed.

"For an instant I couldn't shake off the feeling he was the big one on the monster who was chasing me. I screamed and that brought me fully back, so that I knew where I was and that it was Jake in front of me, but then I couldn't stop screaming and screaming. When I screamed I knew I was *alive*, you see, and I heard my own voice and knew I was home again. Oh God! God! God! It was so horrible!"

And then she stiffened in his arms, stiffened and stood upright and tried to pull away, and her mouth formed a small round pout of pain and terror, and her eyes were closed.

Carter picked her up bodily and carried her hastily to the bed. Working with desperate speed he pried open her rigid jaws and forced two tablets into her mouth, then poured water after them and held her when she coughed and spluttered, held her rigid until the involuntary reflexes forced her to swallow. The drug took effect within minutes and he watched the rigidity fade from her slim body, the breathing ease and become less ragged, until finally she seemed to pass into a normal deep slumber.

When he felt sure she was all right again he sat on the foot of the narrow bed and permitted himself to slowly relax, letting his muscles sag into the posture of weariness and defeat. After a long time he stirred himself and moved slowly to the kitchen, where his food, now cold, was waiting on the table. Suddenly hungry, he sat down and ate hastily, scarcely noticing what passed between his lips. When the hunger pangs were satisfied he left the dirty plates on the table and started pacing the small room, his mind going in dizzy circles, returning constantly to the one central point which there was no denying. He had to find the cause of the illusions and remove them, *now*, while his darling slept. Or there would be no sane awakening.

Four

Something was nagging at the back of his mind, some fragments of the personal nightmare in which he was living. He felt the answer to the weird dreams hung tantalizingly near, that he had all the necessary facts in his possession, if only he could fit and tamp them into place.

He was still pacing, hours later, when Valle stirred and gave a whimper. He went into the bedroom to find her tossing restlessly, making small moaning noises in her throat, and after thinking it over he forced another sleeping tablet down her throat.

When she had relaxed again he stepped out into the night, oblivious of the swarm of hungry insects which instantly pounced on him, and walked to and fro in the small area they called their garden. In the north-west the first grey light of dawn was in the air, paling the sky of its golden moonglow, and he knew it would soon be time for the first shift to report to Administration.

He looked to the south-east, through a small clear area in the heavy woods, and saw a light twinkling far in the distance, a light that appeared to be just off the ground. And suddenly he knew.

It was intuitive, instinctual, more a primal knowledge than reasoned logic, but it came with such deep and certain conviction it left no room for doubts or argument. He *knew*, and acted on the knowledge.

He made a last hasty check on Valle and found her sleeping peacefully, the dark face composed. Then he was out the door and trotting purposefully towards the Changehouse, threading his way through the various paths with sure skill. He reached it just as Canopus came peeping over the horizon, yellow and immense in the distance, and headed for the crawlers parked at the edge of the lake.

He knew he needed a suit, since the interior of the crawlers was often as not hot from shielding leaks, but there was no time. He scrambled inside without touching the bare metal of the hull and seated himself at the control board. He started the pump and felt the movement of the Nak beginning to circulate, and waited in strangled impatience for pressure to build up. Just as the system reached operating temperature he glanced through the port and saw his former partner, Buckley, running frantically towards the crawler, waving his arms. He must have been working slack time, and knew quite well no one had any business in a crawler at that time of the morning.

He ignored Buckley and eased the crawler forward, turning it away from the water and towards the path to Administration. Even at full speed the slow machine could move no faster than ten miles an hour, and he watched his former partner running alongside him for a moment, gesturing frantically, and then ignored him. Buckley swiftly dropped behind.

Buckley would report to Simpson, of course, but it scarcely mattered. There would not be time for anyone to interfere with what he planned to do.

He drove the lumbering vehicle past Administration at a good distance, not even looking that way, and on up the slight rise to the crest of the first gentle hill, then down the slope and through the trees which grew thickly at the bottom. It was ticklish work picking his way for the next few miles, but the crawler had an old-fashioned tank's capacity to go anywhere. In another half-hour he saw the tower ahead and started working his way towards it.

The *Rilli* were abroad even at this time of the morning. He saw several of them staring with pop-eyed amazement at the crawler which had no business near their tower, and when it became obvious he intended to roll straight to it, several of them seized rocks and hurled them at the glass port. He ignored them and a moment later saw some grim-faced guards appear at the base of the tower, armed with bows and arrows. The arrows clattered harmlessly off the window; when they saw there was no chance of stopping him one of the guards, with a cry of despair Carter saw but could not hear, hurled himself under the heavy tracks.

Carter felt the slight bump as the crawler rolled relentlessly on.

The remaining *Rilli* scattered with yells of terror as he wheeled to a stop almost against the towering logs. He hesitated for a moment, then pulled the emergency tool-pack from under the operator's chair and set swiftly to work. It was the labour of but a moment to remove the floorplates, exposing a portion of the cooling system. With hands that trembled slightly he opened the main intake valve where fresh Nak could be added to the system, and jumped back as the hot liquid came boiling out. He hastily undid the hatch locks, reached over to the control board and raised the reactor to full heat, then flipped the hatch back and climbed outside.

The *Rilli* were clustered in a group in front of the machine, including the two *Rilli* with bows. They seemed uncertain just what to do about him, but when he headed for the edge of the clearing at a dead run they made up their minds and started after him.

One arrow went whistling by him and another just over his head before he heard the *Rilli* shout between themselves and the arrows stopped coming. They had decided to take him alive.

He glanced back over his shoulder and saw a small jet of steam rising from the open hatch of the crawler. It curled upward into the still morning air, a grim indication of the terrific heat building up underneath. And he was still dreadfully close.

The *Rilli* were better athletes than he, but his longer legs gave him an advantage they could not overcome. He settled down to a ground-eating lope, not really knowing how long he had, nor how far it was best to be. He was over a mile away, and the nearest pursuer several hundred yards behind, when the explosion came.

The reactor was not an efficient bomb, but the blast did cut through the vast trunks, cut them and lifted the tower several metres into the air before it settled back into a disintegrating heap of wood and rubble.

He felt the change instantly. It was as though he had lived with the sense of presence so long it had become an accepted part of him, no more noticed than the hair on his head or the skin on his hands. It was noticeable by its absence that there had *been* a sense of presence, and now it was gone.

Never, he hoped, to return.

The *Rilli* chasing him had paused in indecision, looking

back on the shattered remnants of their tower. He set off again at a slower trot, and after a moment they decided he was no longer worth chasing and turned back to the smoking ruins. Carter knew they were probably walking towards a fatal dose of radiation, but was too tired to care.

Valle was up and waiting for him, her olive face white with fear. Simpson was there also, and about half the rest of the men on McKeever.

They moved forward purposefully when he came in sight, and he offered no resistance when they took his arms roughly and led him in to face Simpson. The young colonel stared at him sharply, then more intently as he failed to detect the signs of mental breakdown he had evidently expected.

"No, I haven't flipped my wig," said Carter wearily, as the men holding his arms let him sag into a welcoming chair. "Hell, man, can't you *feel* it?"

"Yes, I can tell that something has . . . changed, Carter. I can't quite say what it is, but I do know I feel better." Simpson sat facing Carter and stared intently into the big man's face. "But maybe you'd better start at the beginning. Even if you knew what you were doing you owe us all an explanation. And I can't imagine a reason for not confiding in me sufficiently good enough to save you from a court-martial."

"I thought about it, but there wasn't time. At least, not time enough to convince you. As for starting at the beginning, I'm not sure I can. I'll hazard a guess, and you can see what you think.

"Has it occurred to anyone to wonder where the *Rilli* came from? Who they really are? We've been taking it for granted they evolved on this planet, part of the local fauna. I don't think so any more. I think the *Rilli* are descendants of a spaceship crew, a very large crew which arrived on this planet a thousand years ago. I think their intergalactic ship crashed on this planet, after completing a trip that dwarfs anything of which we've even dreamed. They had some method of cushioning the impact, enough so that a sizable portion of the crew lived through it. Then for reasons at which we can only guess the survivors let their cultural heritage lapse.

"I don't know if they were from a planet where the living was hard and they were corrupted by the soft life here, where food could be had for the taking, or if it was something more subtle, such as a difference in the atmosphere which lowered mental ability. In any case, they went downhill fast, so much so that now even their language has degenerated. Two things they retained, though, were the legends of their people, the tales of race greatness which form the folklore of any outcast group, and the ability to tell those tales, in startling realism, by mental projection."

He paused, and there was a sudden excited outburst from the intent group of listeners. The majority of the men who had already experienced dreams were telling their wives or neighbours how often they had noticed the *Rilli* in them, and how neatly Carter's theory tied together.

"Apparently what had been a pastime, or part-time entertainment feature at home, became a drug, an obsession, on this lonely planet," Carter went on. "As their level of civilization dropped they came to depend more and more on the stories as an escape from reality, until finally the priests were broadcasting day and night. We've seen the result. The *Rilli* walk around in a constant daze, their minds divided between observation of the real world and the ancient sagas they are hearing and seeing inside their heads. It's no wonder they appear stupid."

"It all makes good sense," said Major Chen Yi, who was standing in the listening crowd. "But please tell us how you arrived at your conclusions."

"The clue that put me on the right track was a statement Valle made. She said once that the dream she experienced the night before wouldn't have been so bad if she hadn't tried to understand it. She *couldn't* understand it, the story not being in Earthly terms or Earthly forms. If you just watched it as a meaningless series of experiences and stayed withdrawn you could probably endure it for quite a while. But when you're asleep your mind instinctively *does* try to understand, and the concepts are too alien to be grasped. The result is that the mind begins to lose the ability to distinguish between illusion and reality—and that is insanity."

"The tower, of course, was the home of the priests who remembered and broadcast the great stories," said Simpson thoughtfully. "Those signals we found but couldn't identify were of such short wave-lengths they would be transmitted on a line-of-sight basis only. And the fact they were so weak our best equipment could barely detect them only proves the brain is a better receiver than any machine. But this doesn't fully explain why you chose the drastic method of blowing up the tower, killing the broadcasting priests and ruining one valuable crawler, instead of simply telling me about your suspicions and letting us check them out together."

"Valle couldn't have lasted the night," said Carter simply. "And it hadn't occurred to me those people would be broadcasting on line-of-sight."

"Well, it's too late to worry now," said Simpson with a sigh. "I suppose your contribution to the programme will far outweigh the demerits you're in line for. You'll have to go through a formal court-martial when we get back to Earth, of course, but that shouldn't be for several years now."

He rose to his feet with a grin, the commanding officer again. "We've got a pretty big job ahead of us for the next few days. The *Rilli* will have to be rounded up and moved to a new home far away from here, in case they start broadcasting again, and we've got to come up with some method of making two crawlers do the work of three. Go to bed, Carter, and report for duty tomorrow. Come on, everybody, let's clear out of here and let these people get some rest. They've had a rough night."

After the last unasked guest had gone, Valle came and huddled in his arms and cried a little, but more from relief than tension. He held her quietly until she relaxed, too tired to get up and stagger off to bed.

"We've all learned a lot since yesterday," said Carter thoughtfully, "but we haven't thought about the greatest wonder of all yet. We have, right here on McKeever, citizens of another galaxy. Our planetary biologists back home are going to flip." He eased Valle to the floor, then staggered to the door instead of the bed, and stood staring into the morning sky. He could see nothing but the brightness of the McKeever day, but his imagination reached far beyond the few scattered stars separating Canopus from the lonely immensity of intergalactic space, reached beyond the void of a hundred and fifty-six thousand light-years of emptiness.

Valle was by his side. "One day we'll make that trip ourselves and tell their people of their success. But for now, dear, let me remind you we have the small job of finding what caused the *Rilli* decline, and doing something about it."

"Yes, they have to be picked up," said Carter soberly, turning back inside. He put a heavy arm around her waist. "But that's tomorrow's job."

THE SEA'S FURTHEST END

by

DAMIEN BRODERICK

Mr. Broderick, a new Australian writer to the science fiction medium (but not, by any means, to literature in general) has taken as his theme the wish for Galactic unity, but, as on Earth today, the problem is mainly one of conflicting personalities—or chess pieces on a board. In this respect, someone has to lose.

THE SEA'S FURTHEST END

PROEM

Earth's Golden Age of Empire had come and gone, an exotic flower in the harsh environment of the Galaxy. The age-dark maw of space had waited patiently as Earth's seed exploded across the universe at the opening of the Bright Ages, had bided time while arrogant Man bridged the stars with lines of commerce and allegiance, had reaped satisfaction when the entropy of empire brought Man's dreams crashing into the dust of a million worlds. The universe had chuckled as the heirs of mighty Earth reverted on ten hundred thousand motes in space to primitive tribal civilizations. And again it waited with eternal amusement for the Hunger which would drive men out into the hostile dark between the stars.

The Empire had died of decadence and internecine strife. For basically, empire is an artificial system. Every planet was a self-contained unit, with its own gamut of resources. Certainly, highly organized interstellar trade made for more and cheaper luxury goods. Technique-traders enabled breakthrough discoveries on one planet to benefit the Galaxy. But peace came at the price of freedom, and the Empire fell. After the Wars of Annihilation, Man's spirit was broken and he renounced the stars in the despair common to all Dark Ages.

But the skies had cleared at last. A thousand years had given forty generations time to yearn again for the stars. And this time the groping explorers did not find an empty universe to conquer—on every habitable planet, they met their forgotten brothers, seeded there from Mother Earth twenty thousand years before.

The reavers came, and the missionaries, and the traders, and men dreamed again of Empire. . . .

The Player laughed, and carefully removed his Queen.

One

AYLAN lay on his back in the hush of the garden, his lean figure another shadow in the darkness. Eyes closed, he chewed the end of a grass stem and sucked the sweet juice into his mouth. The Palace was quiet, and the only sounds were the movements of small creatures in the leaves and the long gentle swell of the sea slapping in the distance against the breakwaters. The grass beneath him was soft and smooth, buoyant like the warm sea. Aylan opened his eyes to the sky, and sobbed. Sprinkled in a great blazing halo above his head were the stars Man had once renounced, which Man had now to win back. The sign of Cain was on Man's soul, the mark of war and conquest and bloody murder, and it drove him to empire. Aylan ground his knuckles into his eyes. For those cold shining points of light were his heritage. He was Crown Prince of Loren, son of the man who was gradually making himself Emperor of the Galaxy.

Suddenly the ground seemed uncomfortable beneath him, and Aylan got to his feet. He wandered blindly in the overpowering scent of the trees to the end of the vast garden, down a sandy path to the edge of the sea. The salty acrid smell filled his nostrils and drugged his mind and he crunched across the sand to the edge of the lapping water. The sea was black, an ocean of oil, of tears, and there was no moon. Stars sank from the sky to the end of the sea, out far on the horizon, and drowned in the black salt swell. Aylan had his fur shoes off, and his robe and shirt, before he realized what he was doing, but the lure of the sea was a siren's song, not to be denied. He threw his trousers after the other clothes and walked slowly into the water. It surrounded him, wetting his long hair, carrying him drifting towards the stars on the horizon.

He licked the salt water from his lips and with long powerful strokes swam to the partially submerged breakwater and clambered up on to it. The air was cool after the warm water, and it cleared his head. Above him, the stars were cold as ever, placid, condemning. There was no way of knowing, by looking at them, that men were drowning in one another's blood out there to own them.

There were wars, and rumours of wars. The pounding starships had consolidated victory on the Rim for the Loren system in the days of Aylan's great-grandfather. Now they were pressing into the Centre, into territory where other monarchies and Federations were forming. There, in the more compact systems of Centre where the stars were strewn so close that night was almost brighter than day, the battles were waging between Loren and groups almost as powerful.

The Prince turned his eyes from the stars, and looked back at the glowing palace. In the dark it was hard to see the wild beauty of the stone tracery that was the Imperial Palace on this pleasure world of Nara. Most of the lights were out, for even with the Court retinue present the huge palace was practically empty. Aylan sought out the light of the Emperor's room, but it was not glowing. Probably he would be . . . Yes, Adriel's room was illuminated. The boy closed his eyes against the prick of angry tears. How he hated his father! Adriel. . . . Violently, he shook his head against the impotent anger that raged inside him, and slid once more into the water.

Veret was standing on the balustrade when Aylan reached the palace, outside the encircled cross that marked the chapel. He glanced shrewdly at the Prince as Aylan went by without acknowledging his presence, and ambled along beside the boy.

"Still silent, Aylan?" he commented in his quiet penetrating voice. "Our stay at Nara is almost over, you know, and your mood doesn't seem to have got any better."

Aylan stopped short, and looked with distraught eyes at the quiet brown-robed figure.

"You may be the Emperor's confessor, Father, but I scarcely see why my mood should affect you."

The priest raised one eyebrow and put his hand on Aylan's arm.

"His Majesty has been worried by your sulking and silence," he grunted as he sat on the low marble wall that edged the cloister.

The Prince did not try to hide his bitterness; he flaunted it, gloried in it.

"If His Majesty the Holy Emperor of Loren worried more about his own soul and less about others' the universe would be a happier place." He turned to go, but the priest's constraining hand was on his arm again.

"What is it, boy?" asked Veret, and he was all consolation and strength. "Is it . . . Adriel?"

And suddenly the youth was on his knees, his face buried in Veret's robes, his arms around the priest's legs. The old priest was not surprised at the emotional release. There was strong stuff in the boy but the Emperor had deliberately kept his son reliant on others, denied him the opportunity to stand on his own two feet. Aylan's only trouble, he thought wryly, was emotional immaturity.

In the darkness, Aylan got to his feet again, and he was calmer than he had been for weeks. And colder. In a moment, his face lost its boyish petulance and the grim set of his jaw and mouth betrayed the change his fluid personality had undergone.

"I apologize, Father," he said briskly, and strode rapidly away towards his rooms.

For a moment the old priest followed him with his eyes, startled despite himself by the boy's sudden metamorphosis of character. Then with a grunt and swish of robes he moved back to the chapel, smiling to himself. "There's one more the Emperor Malvara will have to watch out for," he muttered thoughtfully.

Aylan walked across the rich carpets without noticing the ornate beauty of the rooms around him. Here were the strivings and aspirations of men long dead, the beauty captured in straining stone and burning glass, the elegance and grace of a new renaissance. In this palace were represented the dreams and hopes of a hundred Visions, and they went unnoticed by Aylan, for there was death on his mind. He rode the grav-shaft to his floor and saw only the loveliness of Adriel of Corydon and felt only the hate no son should feel for his father.

The walls of his chambers were glowing as he came into them, and he muttered in annoyance at the cleaner who must have left them on. And a quiet voice said, "Good evening, Aylan."

The Prince turned, stunned, to the seat where Milenn was sitting. And then the two men were in one another's arms, clapping each other on the back in happy reunion. Aylan pushed his friend to arm's length and surveyed him. Milenn had changed. No longer was he the carefree debonair nobleman who had grown up with the Prince. Now his handsome face was burned black with the ultra-violet of hot suns. His right cheek was scarred with a needle-burn, and his brow was creased with responsibility. But his laugh was the same, the corners of his strong mouth lifted in happy greeting.

Milenn's survey was no less thorough. He saw a man, not

the boy of twenty-two he had left in the Imperial Palace at Loren a year before. The Prince was slim as ever, but there was muscle under his patrician cloak, and new strength in his blue eyes.

They made a good pair, these two, both tall and slender, but with the resilience of sprung-steel boys. Two who held the destiny of a universe. . . .

"When did you get back?" asked Aylan, as he punched the console for drinks. "I thought you were in Gaunilo at the Centre, under the Duke of Calais."

The service console purred and deposited two smoky-green glasses of a potent beverage from an obscure planet near Nara. Aylan handed one to his friend, extracted a pair of cigars from the pop-up, and sank into a seat opposite Milenn.

The other man was silent for a moment as he lit his cigar, and when he spoke his voice was serious.

"Unfortunately, I'm here as official representative to the Emperor from Jon of Calais. I've just spent two hours in session with His Majesty, and he's considering returning to Loren for a Council Conference. The situation Centreside is simply this: our forces have the Central groups in check, and they're suing for peace. Calais wants to refuse terms and crush them while we have the opportunity. The Emperor is tentatively of the same opinion, and the damned Council will probably agree." He drained his glass in a hasty motion and put his left hand over his eyes, against a pulsing headache.

Aylan sat in silence for a moment, wondering at his friend's upset.

"So, what's wrong with that? It seems perfectly sensible. Don't tell me your loyalties are drifting away from Loren." But he smiled as he said it.

Milenn was not smiling when he looked up. He seemed

upset by his friend's comment. Carefully, he put his cigar down.

"Have you forgotten so soon, Aylan?" he said gently. "Do you remember how we talked, as boys, of history and ideologies, and men's souls? You don't win a man by beating the guts out of him when he's down. These people are ready to admit that Loren is bigger than them. They're almost ready to accept Federation, if they're treated as men and not as animals. Calais will conquer them, yes, wipe out their fleets, but he'll never win their respect and loyalty. Why do you think the last Empire failed? *Because it was built on force and hatred, not affection and loyalty!* We can't let that happen again."

He was silent, and Aylan stared in wonder at this man who saw the future so definitely. And Milenn was right, of course. He always was. The nights and days of their childhood together flooded Aylan's mind, and always Milenn was there, guiding and helping, and always he was right.

"Is there something you want me to do?" Aylan was groping, uncertain of himself in the presence of this sure, confident man.

The sun-burnt warrior sat forward in his chair and examined his hands with elaborate thoroughness. When he spoke, his voice was strained.

"If you still believe in those old-fashioned ideals we used to dream and speak of, there is something. I want you to ask the Emperor to relieve Calais and place you in command of the forces."

The Prince was swaying on his feet, the world ringing in his ears.

"You must be mad!" In a flood, he saw the stars as they had appeared earlier that night, a blazing, cruel, contemptuous halo. He saw the burnt, pocked, blood-stained ships that limped back from the Central theatres of war. He saw his father's laughing, scorning face as he told Aylan that he was taking Adriel of Corydon as diplomatic mistress. He saw himself as a weak dreamer, and knew that he could never lead an army.

Deep in his seat, Milenn sat unmoving. He was prepared for this, had known what to expect. And softly, cutting like an exquisitely sharp knife through the chaos of Aylan's mental turmoil, he spoke.

"Why? Once, you are right, I would have been mad to suggest such a thing. You were weak, for your father had made you so. But not now. Aylan, you are a man. I could tell that as soon as I saw you today. You'll be Emperor one day; you have to learn to face responsibility. And the Centre *must* be saved from butchery."

Aylan was at the console again, and with a flicker of fingers he plunged the room into darkness and set up the Galactic Lens. He was a giant, incredible, standing in nothingness with the suns of the Milky Way burning and flaming around him. Spiralling in a perfect simulacrum of the Galaxy, the Lens filled the room and illuminated it with a dim radiance. The Prince saw Milenn rise to his feet and came forward to the blazing luminescence of Centre.

"Here is the future. A united galaxy, Aylan. Can you imagine what that would mean?" His face shone with a vision, a dedication Aylan could not deny himself. "Federation—that's the dream. Not harshly enforced Empire, but freely accepted peace. And then, who knows? There is intergalactic space, new riches, new technological achievement, perhaps mental and metaphysical evolution. But we must have peace first, and you are the vital key to it."

The whorls of light fled through the darkness, and Aylan was the colossus whose will was to form their shape. He knew, then, that he would have to accept his destiny. Always it is easier to hide in one's shell, to live in the past, to deny the future for the sake of present comforts and assurances, but he could no longer take the easy path. And Aylan felt refreshed, and strengthened.

He went to the console and flicked off the Lens. As the stars faded the walls flowed into life, and they shone in Aylan's eyes as they had shone in his friend's.

"I'll do it," he said, and gripped Milenn's hand in a pact which spelt the end of a universe.

Two

THE long carved oak table in the Royal Refectory was set for breakfast as delicately as ever, despite the fact that the Court retinue would eat only a very hasty meal preparatory to leaving the planet immediately for Loren. Aylan came to the end of the table opposite the Emperor's place, as befitted the heir to the throne, and was glad to see that Milenn was sitting at his right hand. His father and his mistresses had not yet arrived, and Aylan was fidgety. He took the liberty of polarizing the great exterior wall. As the atoms aligned themselves in the field, the wall became one huge window to the gardens of the Palace. Far to the right, Nara's soft yellow sun was still surrounded with the crimson glory of the sunrise. The poet in Aylan was touched, and he was still gazing raptly at the gentle beauty of the morning when Malvara and his women came into the room.

The rough old man was clad in a synsilk crimson and gold toga that displayed his burly strength while lending him an air of respectability he would never really possess in himself. He gave his son a sardonic smile that recognized Aylan's presence, and the Prince returned the nod etiquette demanded. For him the charm of the beautiful morning was shattered and the hatred was gnawing at him again. For at Malvara's right hand sat Adriel of Corydon, diplomatic mistress and sharer of the Imperial bed.

Aylan knew that Malvara was goading him. Since childhood, he had been the focus of a psychological war designed to teach him his subservient position. The Emperor needed an heir; he was afraid that an heir might not need him. So whenever the chance arose, Malvara crushed his son and topped off the lesson with the unspoken moral: *I'm on top, boy, and don't forget it!*

Adriel had been the last lesson, but Malvara had miscalculated. Aylan was not cowed. It was the last straw, and the fear and self-disgust turned to cold hatred. Aylan knew that he would have to kill his father.

Adriel was the lovely daughter of the ex-Tyrant of Corydon. The scientists of that Rim system had reached their finest achievement in her, for she was genetically designed for beauty, intelligence, and . . . something else. Geneticists gave her a talent, a wildly improbable gift, and even they did not know what it would be.

She was an Emote.

"Chameleon-like" was the inevitable adjective, but it wasn't accurate. Adriel could control her Emoting. It was a defence-mechanism, but it was more. It was a talent, and she could use it at will.

Of course, everybody loved her. In a fraternal, helping fashion. Her subconscious knew better than to Emote in a sexually attractive manner. She had no desire to be raped by every male who came within her Emotive range. But for Aylan, the quiet son of her father's conqueror, she had felt the stirrings of love.

They had been like children, in their new discovery. Their love was sunrise and the scent of roses and the soft breath in the sheets. She drew the beginnings of manhood from the frightened adolescent who was Aylan, and their love was a burgeoning flower.

For Malvara, it was unthinkable that his son should have such a victory. So Adriel became his diplomatic mistress.

She could, of course, have used her Emotive talent to breed horror, or disgust, or terror of her in Malvara's mind, but the Emperor was not a fool and there were ten heavy cruisers in orbit around each planet in the Corydon system.

So Aylan sat at the end of a long table, his fist clenched hard on the fork at the sight of the veiled nun-like form at his father's right hand. Feed a hatred enough fuel for long enough, and hold it under pressure, and one day it will destroy either the hater or the hated. Aylan toyed with food he could not eat, and knew that he would not be the one to die.

Council was in session when the Court returned to the Imperial City at Loren. His Majesty, the Holy Emperor Malvara, Lord Master of Loren and the Galaxy, came into the vast arching monument which was the Council Chambers and took his place on the levitated throne six feet above the marble floor. The Council stood until he was seated, then found their places in silence. Malvara rarely called on the Council for advice in policy decisions.

The grizzled old man looked even more like a gorilla in his luminously white cloak. Dismissing the trivia of formalities, Malvara came straight to the point.

"My lords of Loren. In the long and bloody war we have been waging with the Central alliances, we have ever sought to bring them to allegiance with our glorious empire. Now, through the brilliant spatial and planetside command of Jon of Calais, Loren has the major powers begging for terms of peace. Calais has sent to me in the able hands of Count Milenn of Danak a request for permission to reject all terms and wipe out the enemy while they are in this weakened condition. Of course, this would result in antagonism towards Loren for some generations, but the question which must be resolved today is: would this course of action best serve the interests of the Empire of Loren, or should we accept terms and run the risk of new revolt in the near future?"

His glance ranged the floor of the Chambers, and there was a moment of silence before the low hum of discussion began among the Members. These oldsters were still barbaric in their thinking, but they were shrewd enough to realize that here was a decision of overwhelming importance for the future of the Galaxy.

Malvara waited restlessly on his floating throne for ten minutes while the Members conferred hastily with one another, and then called for the first Speaker in Consultation to take the rostrum.

Even as the first Speaker came forward, there was a stir near the Family Entrance, and Aylan entered the Chambers. Garbed in the iridescent purple and white fur of the Imperial House he was a striking figure, and the maturity of purpose in the set of his jaw startled Malvara considerably. From his lofty position the Emperor watched the unprecedented entry of his son into the Council and for the first time he felt afraid.

Craning necks and furtive whispers showed that the Members of Council in Consultation were surprised too. The first Speaker took another step towards the rostrum, hesitated, and then waited for further developments, a ludicrously unhappy figure in the aisle.

The trim figure of the Prince continued straight to the limits of the Protection-field surrounding the Emperor, and made ceremonial obeisance directly before Malvara.

"I crave the pardon of the Emperor and his Council," he began, still facing Malvara, "for this intrusion, and I beg leave to take advantage of my right as Royal Family to address the topic."

There was nothing Malvara could legally do to prevent Aylan speaking, so he gave his consent as graciously as he could. As he watched his son mount the rostrum, his mind whirled in a crazy turmoil. For twenty-two years he had been pressuring Aylan, nudging, kicking, hurting, pushing him, with the express purpose of making it psychologically impossible for the Prince to take the kind of action he was taking now. The sweat of fear dribbled down Malvara's back, and it took a conscious effort to restore his normal sardonic calm.

"Truth is more than an attitude of mind," Alan was saying. "Federation is our goal. Empire is the means of getting there, but it is not an end in itself. We all know what happened to Man in the Galaxy last time Empire turned from a temporary tool to an encrusted system. Oh, I know it sounds like treason, and even to some, heresy, but the Empire is only a waystation to a bigger dream."

He paused, and he felt the strength of conviction running through him. The Emperor, he noticed, was stock-still in his throne, perhaps hearing his death-knell. Nowhere was there a sound or a movement; the clock of time had slowed.

"You cannot destroy a man's family and expect him to love you. This is a truism, and it isn't important when you're dealing with Empire. Love has no essential place in an Imperial world. But in a galaxy where men are free and really equal, in the Federation which I hope to God is the dream of all of us, love is *the* essential. We cannot afford to alienate the Centre by brutal mass-murder. For the dream is closer than we could ever have hoped. As the Emperor has told you, the Central states have sued for peace. Here is our chance for peaceful Empire, and eventually for peaceful Federation."

Blood racing at his own audacity, Aylan stepped from the rostrum and moved through the deadly silence of the Chamber until he was before his father's throne again.

"My father, Emperor Malvara. You have heard what I have said. I have spoken of theory. Now I ask you to let me put theory to the test. Transfer command of Central operations from Calais to myself. Let me go to the rulers of the Hub with peace, and I swear that the Empire will not suffer the tragedies which will inevitably befall it if Jon of Calais is allowed his bloody way."

In the vast chiaroscuro of the room, the moment of timelessness stretched on and on. The tall, slim figure of the Prince was a flare that burned to the Emperor's feet. Malvara was a cold angry statue, his lips pressed into a thin white scar, his thick black-haired hands gripped in a death lock on the ornate throne. And then the timelessness was gone, with a great croak of a laugh from the Emperor. His head went back, and the laughter rang through the hall. Mocking, amazed, angry. Aylan went limp, for he knew that he had failed and now he must do what he did not want to do.

Malvara's face was a mask of hate and his voice was all sarcasm.

"Were you not my son, dear Aylan, you would surely die for what you have spoken. Your noble sentiments have indeed turned to treason in your addled brain. And you want the command! I would rather give it to the fool who amuses my court. My poor little boy! From the company of women and children you would venture into the domains of men?" He spat, a great gout that landed at Aylan's feet. "Now go home and forget that this unfortunate incident ever happened."

He raised his eyes to the Council, the numb group of men who were trapped in a drama that was too big for them to understand. Without pausing, completely ignoring the Prince, he spoke to the white-haired men in the ranked levels.

"I have decided. Calais is to go ahead—the Central kings shall die, for the Empire can brook no competition."

With a flourish, Malvara wrapped his robes around himself and brought the huge throne to the floor. Aylan stood like a dummy, a clay doll, as the Emperor walked past him to the Family Entrance. As the Entrance slid open, life suddenly surged into him, and he spun round towards the Emperor.

"Wait!" His roar rang down the hall, and Malvara made an elaborate show of halting on one foot and turning slowly with a sardonic expression on his face.

"Aylan," he said, almost gently, "I have told you to go home."

But the Prince was striding forward now, and he was cold with fear for the moment of death had come.

"Malvara," cried Aylan in a voice that chilled the Members of the Council with its lack of all humanity, "as heir-apparent, under the Law of Yusten the First-emperor, I plead fair cause and call you out to the Duel."

And here, thought Malvara with a sudden weariness, is my life and its meaning.

"I accept, of course," said the thick grizzled man and, turning his back on the Prince, left the Chambers.

The Player studied his Board, the billions of pieces, the vast shifting complexity of it, and saw that his King was in danger. Carefully, he shifted his Queen and sat back. The Game was nearing its end.

Yusten had been a legend in his own time, and in the spreading Loren Empire his name had grown in proportion to the number of years which had passed since his death. His life had followed the classic pattern of a popular hero. Born amid the turmoil of the resurging empires, he had risen in the ranks of the soldiery until he had control of the Loren system. Tall and good-looking like Aylan, thickly muscled like his son Malvara, and with the profound insight given only to a few, he had been a popular hero who had made Loren into the potential Empire Malvara had inherited on his death.

Barbaric, cultured, man of the sword, legalist—this strange and powerful figure had left behind him as his towering monument the Laws of Yusten. Prime among these were considerations concerning the internal politics of the Imperial Family. In a primitive fusion of law and blood, he had instituted the Judicial Duel. And for the first time since its legal inception, the trial by duel was to determine whether father or son should rule the Empire.

Milenn sat back in the luxurious comfort of a pneumo-couch and chewed his thumb worriedly. One of the paradoxes he had discovered in his strange odyssey was that violence is often the necessary path to peace. He watched Aylan checking his weapons for the duel, and knew that his strange destiny was coming to its fruition.

"The thing that has me worried," grunted Aylan, as he strapped his mini-load force shield under his cloak, "is the fact that my father has had live-duel experience. It could be the factor which wins him the Duel."

The automatic doorkeep buzzed, and a moment later a valet came into the room with a positron blaster freshly energized. With a word of thanks, Aylan took it from him, and weighed the weapon in his hand. Then, satisfied, he placed it in the jewel-encrusted holster strapped across his stomach. He looked at his watch and saw that there were only eighteen minutes left before the Duel.

"Come on," he said to his friend. "I want to test this damned thing out again in the Range before I go."

Together, they walked down the wide carpeted corridor to the Firing-range. The weight of metal in Milenn's pocket bounced against his thigh, and he was in an agony of indecision as to whether he ought to take it out and give it to Aylan. It would mean deception in the Duel, but there were more important things involved than honesty with a man one was trying to kill.

The door to the Range slid open as they approached it. Aylan went in first and walked on to the floor of the vast room, while Milenn raised a heavy-power force shield around himself.

"Are you safely covered?" asked Aylan, and when Milenn nodded, the Prince activated the Range. Immediately the room went pitch-black; a perfect simulacrum of the real Duel Hall. For a moment, Aylan's force-shield flared into life, a violet nimbus that illuminated him in the darkness. And with a *hish*, a long bolt of energy snapped at him. His reaction had been fast; as soon as his shield had come on, he had thrown himself to the ground and rolled feet away from where he had been. The energy bolt thrown at him by the robot Enemy hissed past him, and before the Enemy had time to fire again he had snapped a shot of his own at the source of the bolt. There was no chime from the Strike-Indicator, so obviously he too had missed. His shield flickered out, and he was unprotected again.

Cautiously in the dark, as silently as he could, he crept towards the other end of the Range. Suddenly the nimbus of the Enemy's shield flickered on, and Aylan's bolt hissed towards the android. His aim was poor, and he missed by feet. And then a shot caught him with a jolt that threw him off his feet. Simultaneously, the Indicator chimed loudly, and the lights went on.

Dropping the heavy shield, Milenn went out on to the Range and helped Aylan to his feet. The Prince had dropped his gun, and as he got up he picked up the weapon.

"That," he said smiling ruefully, "would have been that, if the robot had had a real power gun. I only hope the Emperor has slowed up a bit on his reactions since he programmed for that robot."

Milenn's mind was made up. When he had seen Aylan caught by the bolt, he had realized that he could afford to leave nothing to chance. Quickly, he drew a small, heavy tube of anodized metal from his pocket, and handed it to Aylan.

"Look, Aylan," he said gravely, "the Galaxy can't afford to have you killed today. We're just going to have to use a little duplicity."

The tube was cold in Aylan's hand, and he looked at it in puzzlement. It was like nothing he had ever seen before. He raised his eyes in question at Milenn.

"It's an Old Empire weapon," said the Count, grimly. "It's called a stasis gun, and it was probably the most powerful weapon the Ancients ever developed. I'm not sure how it works, but I can assure you it does work most effectively. Somehow it brings everything in its range into minimal stasis, so that all the constituent atoms are brought to the one energy level. You'll have to use it if you want to come out of this duel alive."

As he spoke, he took the tube from Aylan's numb hands and inserted it skilfully under the energy pack of the positron blaster. Its weight balanced out nicely, and Milenn handed the gun gingerly back to the Prince.

"Use the blaster as you ordinarily would, and for God's sake don't get shot before you have a chance to use it. The field is big enough to ensure that your enemy is destroyed even if you only have his general location."

He looked at his watch. There were three minutes left before the Duel. Aylan was still looking dumbly at the blaster.

"An Old Empire weapon?" He was shaking his head. "Where did you get it? It must be a thousand years old."

"It is, and there's a long story connected to it. But at the moment, you have a duel to win."

Candles flickered in the chapel and bathed the altar in a roseate glow. Veret finished the Mass, blessed the two combatants, and rose to give the sermon. His aged face was worn with worry, and as he spoke the tears ran unashamedly down his face. To him at least, the Duel carried a more transcendental aspect than the future of the Empire. Today, a father would kill a son, or a son would claim his father's life.

Finally, the service was over, and the retinue moved from their pews, out of the incense-laden air to the clean freshness of the garden cloister. Sombrely, the procession moved to the Duelling Range, Malvara and Aylan leading the way. For Aylan, it was like walking through thick glutinous treacle. His breath was coming hard, and his heart was pounding with a frightening intensity. Death was no terror to him, not any longer. Rather it was the fear of the unnatural that gripped his limbs and tried to hold him back. His hatred for his father was gone now, in the face of patricide. Of course, he could not lose. Nothing manufactured in these barbarian days could withstand an Old Empire weapon. Sweat beaded his face, and then the retinue was in the Duelling Range.

All except Aylan and the Emperor moved behind the heavy-power shields at the side of the range, and the two were left facing one another. For a heart-choking moment Aylan wanted to cry out, to put a stop to the Duel. The old craggy face of his father swam in his eyes, and he opened his mouth and . . .

The lights were gone. Alone. It hadn't been like this on the robot Range. Here he could be killed. Dead. Surcease. He swallowed, and seemed to hear the dry *gulp* echo down the Range. He was surprised to find that he had crept noiselessly along the wall to the right. Heavy in his arms, the blaster was a reassurance. Now there was the waiting game, the gamble. Whose shield would come on first? If it was his, he would dive forward, and to the left, roll forward and to the right. If it was his father's, he would fire straight at the after image. That is, if Milenn was right. If the stasis beam was wide. What if the bloody old thing blew up? Too late to worry about that now.

And the nimbus was around him. He didn't move. Not for a split second, and that was long enough. Even as he dived, Malvara's energy stream streaked at him and caught the violet nimbus. The shock was ten times as great as the token jolt of the robot Range, and if the mini-shield hadn't been there the positron stream would have torn him apart. As it was, he was hurled backwards and he lost his grip on the blaster. It clattered away across the floor.

The neuronic blast of the feedback as the field neutralized the positron stream held him crippled. Desperately he wanted to retch, and desperately he controlled himself, for the slightest noise would invite another blast from Malvara. Shaking uncontrollably, he got to his hands and knees and searched around for the blaster. His hand touched something hard and cold, and he had the blaster in his hands again. Relief and reaction swept over him, and he sat on the floor cradling the blaster, as nerveless as a rag doll. Malvara's nimbus flickered on, and Aylan still sat on the floor hugging the weapon to himself.

As the Emperor hurled himself to one side, Aylan straightened up in the darkness and aimed his blaster. Before he could fire, the violet flame was gone. Without any thought at all, he extrapolated the direction of his father's leap, and pressed the activator of his blaster.

For a moment the room was brighter than day. A great funnel of light leapt from Aylan down the room, surrounding the fallen Malvara and bathing the back wall. Then the light was gone, but the Emperor was blazing like a torch, and a circle of the wall and floor behind him was red-hot. Slowly, his features melted into a ghastly caricature of his normal sardonic expression. With a gentle sighing sound, his body collapsed into a slag of hot liquid which mingled with the material of the floor and walls which had been caught in the field. Through the new hole in the wall, a calm breeze wafted in and carried to Aylan the scent of sweet flowers and burnt flesh. And there was no reason any more to control his retching.

THREE

AYLAN walked in a sack-cloth robe down the gaunt pillared solitude of the cathedral, and he was lost in a drift of years and incense. Alone he walked, tall and strong in the century-old beauty of the vast cathedral, until he stood in the arc of the altar's great stone tracery. Here there was hope, though death and hatred had preceded it and would surely return again in the future. But there was no hatred here, only a tired age and a silent mighty blessing in stone, and somewhere waiting for him, Adriel.

Above him flamed the colours of the stained glass windows, and before him were the Archpriest and his lace-robed acolytes. With measured care, Aylan stepped forward to the lowest level of the altar, and prostrated himself on the floor. The voice of the Archpriest came through a haze of unreality and the acolytes were the whole world chanting.

"Is this the man Aylan, heir-apparent, who claims the crown?"

"Aye, this is the man."

"Is he cleansed of the evils of pride and avarice, worthy to receive the Imperial dignity?"

"Aye, though he is the dust of the earth, the crown must be his."

"Then stand, Aylan, and ascend to the altar of God."

It is difficult to rise from a prostrate position with dignity, but Aylan had been trained for this moment for years. He dipped his hands into the bowl of clear oil an acolyte held, and the Archpriest carefully cleaned them again with a white cloth. Then he gently unfastened the clasps on the ugly dun robe Aylan had been wearing. One of the priests took the robe from his shoulders, and the Prince stood like one transformed before the altar. Glistening white, flaming with precious stones, his tunic did justice to the office he was assuming.

He took his place on the great throne, and the Archpriest turned to the people.

"Here is Aylan of Loren." The crown was in his gnarled old hands, a miracle of beauty in metal and the glowing nimbus of a force shield. Slowly and majestically, he placed it on Aylan's head.

"In the name of God and the Christus, I name him Emperor. Do ye give him love and allegiance."

But, though his words were amplified through the cathedral, no one heard them. The roars and cheers of the crowd drowned everything in a spontaneous outburst of approval that sent tears coursing down Aylan's face, and he knew that he had not been wrong in accepting his destiny.

The scent-drenched garden of the Imperial Palace was no less enchanting than the one Aylan had wept in at Nara. How could it be less for there Aylan had not had Adriel beside him, laughing with her hand in his. He stopped and looked at her, drinking in the beauty of her face. In the golden afternoon, she was a rose-petal, delicate, desirable beyond words. And without words he enfolded her in his arms, savouring her lips, and their love was a soaring joy that held them wondering at the universe. They lay down on the grass, and night came in gold and red and twilight blue. There was the scent of leaves, and night came wonderfully, among the throng of dark trees.

"Can we do it?" whispered Aylan, and Adriel followed his gaze to the sprinkling sky. "Can we make a Federation from them? It seems an impossible dream, and yet—Milenn has gone."

"When he comes back, we will know." She looked at his face, and kissed away his frown. "No, he does not have to come back. I know now. You can do it."

Her simple faith was touching, and contagious. Aylan's hand ruffled her hair, and he closed his eyes.

"Of course we can, dearest," he said drowsily, "of course we can. . . ."

The sub-radio cracked viciously with the flux of the terrible energies that raged between the stars. But it carried Milenn's voice, unmistakable, and he was angry.

"Calais' power has gone to his head." The Count's voice dipped and roared in the Communications-room. "He refuses to hand over command, and he is already making advanced preparations to planet-bomb the two largest Central systems." His voice faded completely, and technicians twisted knobs frantically to hold the carrier wave. Sub-space transmission was always a risky proposition, and Milenn's ship was still almost five thousand parsecs away.

Aylan paced furiously up and down in the small room, as angry as Milenn to see his dreams close to destruction because of mutiny within his own ranks.

". . . only one thing to do," came in Milenn's voice. "Fit up the Imperial Guard force with stasis weapons and hightail it in here to Centre before Jon wipes out all hope of peaceful Federation."

"But good God, man," roared Aylan, "you say you hardly know the principle of the stasis field yourself. How could we possibly crack the idea in time?"

There was a time lag of some seconds, and Milenn's voice crackled back through the strange universe of sub-space.

". . . my rooms in the Palace, there are blueprints of the device. Like . . . pire devices, it's extremely simple in design, getting its potency from total conversion of energy. You could have the projectors made in the ship's workshops on your way in here. I'll meet the Guard at Leith in two days, so you'll have to snap straight to it."

Aylan felt no resentment at the way his friend had taken control of the situation. Certainly, Milenn knew more about the position Centreside, and he spoke with a new authority that the Emperor did not think to question.

"Very well." His voice travelled almost instantaneously to the hurtling Ambassador ship. "Although I doubt whether we will be in time. . . ."

"Good luck, Aylan." Milenn's voice had softened. "You just have to get here," but he did not sound as convinced of success as Adriel had the previous night.

Hanging in orbit above the Imperial planet, the Emperor's special Guard was *the* crack unit of the Loren Navy. Two heavy cruisers, mile-long monoliths whose fields could withstand a nova-bomb, and whose armament could wipe out a system, but whose relatively limited velocity made them defensive rather than tactical. More immediately valuable, the light cruisers and the two-man attack minnows. Now, five hours after Milenn's dramatic message, the ships' drives were idling hot while Aylan made his last preparations in connection with the stasis projectors. Without them, such a light task force would be little use against Calais' huge war Navy, and the best engineers on Loren were gradually going crazy trying to apply millenium-old diagrams to lathe and metal. The tiny heavy projector which had won Aylan his duel was X-rayed and dissected and put together again for four hours until finally the engineers solved the diagrams. From then on, there was only the sheer mechanical work of devising efficient and rapid ways of constructing heavy-duty projectors en route to Leith.

Five hours and seventeen minutes after the message, the new Emperor was lifting in a shuttle to the flagship of the Guard. With him were three engineers, a multitude of diagrams and a good-as-new Old Empire stasis blaster.

Normally, sub-space jumping is a boring business, but the two-day trip to Leith was scarcely time enough for the machine-shops in the light cruisers to turn high-tensile steel into the long innocent-looking tubes which, when coupled to heavy-power fields, would be capable of destroying an armada of ships. And would have to.

Leith was growing into a verdant globe in the viewscreen when word came to the flagship that the last of the projectors had been installed. The Guard had re-entered normal space on the rim of the Leith system and were flashing towards the rendezvous planet on solar drive. In the control-room of the flagship *Ascaux*, Thony Lord Hardt lit Aylan's cigar with a steady hand, and watched in quiet amusement as his Emperor proceeded to chew the end of the cigar to shreds.

"Sit down, Excellency," he suggested. "There's at least an hour to planet-fall, and pacing up and down like a caged puma will only wear you out." He was a giant of a man, this Commander of the Emperor's Guard, and a great black beard covered most of his craggy face. He had not been unhappy to hear of Malvara's death, for he had never liked the cruel, hard Emperor, and this earnest young man appealed to him. The thought of the imminent civil war troubled him, but in the two days out to Leith Aylan had managed to transmit some of his tremendous enthusiasm for the necessity of peaceful Federation to everyone with whom he had come in contact. Lord Hardt repressed his smile and scratched the black thatch of his head instead.

Aylan released a ragged sigh and collapsed into a seat. He had lost a considerable amount of weight in the two-day trip, transmuted into the nervous energy he so liberally expended.

"Why is it, Thony, that the path of peace must run with blood?" There was agony on his finely featured face. "Why, when self-preservation is so obviously one of the primal urges in Man, must he be ever trying to commit racial suicide? Perhaps there is indeed some Original Sin that drives social man to self-slaughter."

"I'm no great philosopher, Excellency," said the bearded Commander, "but I'm sure you're wrong. Look at history. There has always been a predominant current towards peace. I think you'll find that the war-mongering element is limited to a very few malcontents, though God knows they're usually powerful enough." He stubbed out the butt of his cigar. "And there are the great mass of soldiery who, like myself, have no love for war yet fight to protect themselves and other peacelovers. Maybe 'the meek shall inherit the earth', but unfortunately it'll only be after they've destroyed all the violent ones."

He chuckled and heaved his giant frame from the chair.

"I suggest that we get on to the sub-radio and find out if Count Milenn has anything new which will set your mind at ease."

Leithside, Milenn knew nothing fresh, but expressed his opinion that Calais' preparation for wholesale massacre must be nearly completed. By the time the Guard ships reached the green globe of Leith, Aylan was almost physically ill with strain. Lord Hardt was visibly relieved when the tiny silver needle of the Ambassador ship intercepted with the fleet, and Milenn came aboard the flagship. The presence of Aylan's tall space-burnt friend calmed the Emperor considerably, and he was able to settle down to the complex business of planning his approach to Calais.

"The rebel forces are obviously in a poor political position," mused Milenn. He, Aylan, and Thony sat at the conference table in the Emperor's small luxurious stateroom. "Aylan is a popular figure at the moment, as Calais' spies must have ascertained by now. He must be banking on a *coup d'état*, so we can at least hope that he will have diverted his forces temporarily from the problem of exterminating the Central systems to the more pressing matter of removing Aylan."

"That's true." Hardt was doodling absently on a sheet of paper, but his mind was as sharply concentrated on the problem as an electronic computer. "Duke Jon may be a megalomaniac but he's no fool. He won't be expending forces in wiping out any of the Central systems if doing so leaves him at a disadvantage in facing us. If he destroys us now, cleaning up the Centre will be no harder for him later than it is now. Whereas, if he wipes out the Central groups now and gets killed by our fleet as a result, his orgy of destruction will have brought him no gain."

"I think you're forgetting two things," warned Aylan. He sat back in his seat and looked grimly at first one man and then the other. "First, Calais has a pretty vast army out there, and since he doesn't know about our secret weapon, the Guard won't appear as much of a challenge to him. He has enough ships to be able to divert twice our number to deal with us while still going ahead with the general massacre."

There was a moment when the only sound was the hum of the air-purifiers; his point had struck home.

"Second, Calais is a bitter man, and as you said, Thony, a megalomaniac. If he does realize that his destruction is inevitable, he may indulge in a widespread slaughter as a kind of insane revenge."

Through the featureless dark of sub-space, the task-force sped at a fantastic multiple of the speed of light, in a race with time to cross a quarter of a galaxy. And inside the

Ascaux, three men struggled to solve a problem on whose solution hung the destiny of a race, and though they were not aware of it, the destiny of a universe.

The Board was a billion scintillating lights, a trillion moving pieces. Again, the King was in danger, and the Queen was in no position to help. The Player moved his Pawns. The Game was nearly over.

Across the heart of the Galaxy, the Imperial fleet of Loren hung like a fine-spun net, holding impotent the forces of the Central systems. Anani, Kiel, Ghatoos, Blucher, Menai, the proud young systems of the Hub, held under the iron hand of Jon of Calais.

In the fleet's flagship, *Loren*, the iron hand of Jon of Calais was wrapped solidly around a glass of an infamous high-proof beverage. The Duke was a hard, bitter man, and alcohol was the only weakness he permitted himself. He had reason for his basic misanthropy; in one of Nature's whimsical jests, he had been born with no legs. He had never forgiven the rest of mankind for having two more limbs than he, and it was almost inevitable that with his brilliant strategic mind he would turn to that profession where he could legally take bloody revenge on mankind *en masse*.

He sat hunched on the plastic-padded grav-plate that served him for legs, a black hawk in his form-fitting Navy overalls. The liquor burned down his throat and added fire to his hatred for the young upstart who was trying to ruin his plans. In the viewscreen that covered half the wall the stars of the Hub blazed like an inferno of jewels. Calais unconsciously licked his lips as he looked at them, and his grip tightened on the goblet.

There was a chime from the video, and its bland screen dissolved into the head and shoulders of his Chief of Staff.

"Sir, we've just received a message missile from one of

your agents on Loren. The new Emperor left Loren three days ago with the Imperial Guard, with the intention of forcing you to relinquish command. The task-force with the Emperor on board should probably arrive here within a day or so."

"With the Guard, hey?" Calais looked more than ever like a great brooding bird of prey, peering down his long nose. "Now what could he expect to accomplish with such a token force against what I've got here. I've got to have time to think about this. Suspend activity on the preparations for planet-bombing for the moment; we may need those ships for a more immediate purpose. Thank you, Admiral, I'll get in touch with you." He flicked off the screen and it faded again into translucence.

Why would Aylan send such a token force indeed? Of course, the bulk of the fleet was out here at Centre, but had Aylan wanted he could have brought the whole of the defence force. Hmm. The new Emperor was, of course, a moral weakling, thanks to his father's careful training. Did he then expect the forces to be handed over to him just because of a personal appearance? It seemed hardly possible, but the milk-sop Aylan was naïve in the ways of real men.

The Duke made his decision, and flicked on the video again.

"Admiral, hold developments here as they are at the moment. I think I'll take a small task-force vessel to deal with our impetuous young Emperor."

Jon of Calais smiled to himself. Events were turning out better than he could ever have hoped. Rid himself of Aylan now, beat the Central fools to their knees, and then. . . .

The stars blazing in the viewscreen were a song of worship to his name.

All Aylan's questions were resolved ten hours later when,

still in sub-space, the ship's detectors revealed a fleet of unknown size approaching from the direction of Calais' base of operations. Thony advised against the sub-radio communication with the other fleet until they broke radio silence first.

"If Calais is with them," said Milenn, as the three men stared in semi-darkness at the green traces on the detector screens, "and knowing his power complex he's sure to want to be in on the kill, we can try negotiations first, and if he isn't interested we'll have to use the stasis fields."

Lord Hardt's practised eye studied the screen intently for a moment, and he voiced his opinion that the other fleet was only two or three times as big as the Guard.

"Then probably the rest of the war-force is maintaining the *status-quo* Centreside." Aylan looked across to Milenn. "If we destroy Calais, will the rest of the fleet come back under Imperial command?"

His friend gave a short snort that could have been a chuckle, but there was no humour in it.

"Most of them are unaware of their rebel status. It is the high-ranking officers who have fallen under Jon's spell that we must watch. But I think that with Calais gone they will lick your feet as though nothing ever happened."

A speaker squawked, and an adjutant's voice informed the Emperor that the approaching ships had made sub-radio contact with the Guard.

The communications-room was humming with the static of deep space when the trio arrived to take the message from Calais' ship. Lights flickered from banks of meters as the ship's cryotronic computer struggled to hold the carrier wave that was propagating across the strange not-world of sub-space. Five hours and over three thousand light-years apart, the two fleets were connected by a magic not understood properly even by those who used it.

For the first time since his adolescence, Aylan heard the

deep handsome voice of Duke Jon of Calais. Torn and distorted though it was by the static of sub-space, the compelling voice conjured up pictures of a clear-eyed golden-haired god, a cord-muscled, beneficent Grecian deity. Here, thought Aylan, is the secret of his power over men, and it was incredibly hard to substitute the image of a hawk-faced maniac for that of the glowing god.

"You realize, of course," the golden voice was saying, "that I cannot accept you as Emperor. I have had no word from the Council, and I am left with the inevitable conclusion that you have murdered your royal father and seized the reins of power illegally."

Aylan glanced helplessly at Milenn, and the Count took the microphone from him.

"Listen, Calais," he grated. "I came to you as authorized legate of both your Emperor Aylan of the line of Yusten, and the Council, and I left with you documents which ordered you to relinquish your command at the Centre to the new Emperor. If you continue in this insane mutiny you can expect only execution, and dishonour to your name. If, even at this late hour, you acquiesce in the Emperor's orders your name will be cleared as acting in good faith. Make up your mind; the time has passed for childish lies."

The handsome voice was cold now, with a hard, cruel edge, like a god admonishing his creatures.

"True enough," it said, "the time is past for games. I have with me a force three times as large as your own, and behind me I have the whole Imperial offence-force. I intend to rule the Galaxy, *Emperor,* and unless you turn and run home like the scared mouse you are, I'm afraid I will have to kill you myself."

White and shaking with anger, Aylan snatched the microphone from Milenn's hand and roared his fury across the light-years.

"I return your ultimatum to you, carrion, and formally remove from you your command, your Imperial rank and privileges, and your right to life. Come, rebel, and discover what death is like at first hand." There was a loud click as he broke contact with the on-coming ships in one violent sweep of his hand.

Five hours and eleven minutes later the two fleets intercepted, and after the hours of tension the battle was almost terrifyingly anti-climactic. The Guard flipped out into real space in a half-moon formation, the horns towards Galactic Centre. They were near the centre of a globular cluster, and the stars hung coldly about them like a million teardrops, a million celestial diamonds. Seconds later the larger task-force from Centre precipitated into space in a sphere-formation. Jon's ship hung in the centre of the sphere, a heavily-armed cruiser sitting in the safest position.

Aylan's flagship sat on one of the horns and inside her control-room three men sat watching the other fleet, hoping against all reason that there would be no need to use the stasis fields. A green flare silently flashed from the rebel fleet, and engulfed one of the Guard ships in a titanic incandescence of energy. The ship's lights dimmed as the force-shield struggled to neutralize the flare, the momentarily under-powered stabilizers tossed the ship crazily, and then the lights came on again. The shield had held. In the control-room of the *Ascaux*, Aylan realized that the fleet could not withstand such a one-sided battle for long. Reluctantly, he gave the order to activate the stasis projectors.

Space was a vast white glare, a ghastly effulgence of death. For an eternal instant. Then there was only the star-filled darkness, and sixty pink glowing drops of molten metal, plastic, flesh. . . .

The whole encounter had taken less than twenty seconds.

Four

Of all the Ancients' wondrous works, the most awesome and permanent was Prima. The Old Imperial planet, a world—to look at it—dedicated to loveliness, where the grandeur of Nature under the restraining guidance of Man sang an everlasting hymn of praise to beauty. Lifted in an unimaginable engineering feat from a cold dark sun which had held it trapped in the death of night for aeons, it had been placed in orbit around the barren white sun which stood like a virgin Queen in the centre of the Galaxy. And under the inspiring genius of the hand of Man, Prima had flowered, her oceans had foamed again, her mountains had learned anew to cry at a living sun.

A monument to beauty, to Man. But this was as nothing compared with the reality which lay beneath the skin of the planet. For twenty, thirty miles beneath the surface, Prima was honey-combed with the nests of men. Here had been the administrative centre of the Galactic Empire. Here was the Imperial Palace, in the planet that men had placed at the centre of the Galaxy. And here, in tiers of metal and superfluid helium, was the Computer that girdled the circumference of Prima.

But now the Computer was dead, the cryotronic dance of its memory banks stilled a millenium before in the shock of the civil war which had shaken the Galaxy back to barbarism. Most of the vast area of office- and living-space, where once had teemed a planetary population of bureaucrats, had crashed and fallen in that cataclysmic war, but the Old Council Hall had been miraculously untouched, and the king of the new Monarchy of Kiel had made it his own. And relinquished it to his conquerors from Loren.

Milenn felt a heart-clutching sense of foreboding as he stood beside his Emperor and Empress in the garden of Nature that stretched to the horizon in waves of green and yellow. In a few short minutes, they would descend the grav-shaft to the Council Hall, and if everything went well, the Galaxy would see for the first time—Federation! The wild elation that was obviously gripping Aylan had completely left Milenn, and he was swamped with a nightmare conviction of unreality. It was as though the blackness before his eyes was really there, the singing in his ears, the head-pounding blood. . . .

"Aylan," he cried, in a terror that was almost childlike. For a moment the world spun around him, and then he was leaning on the solid assurance of his friend's arm.

"Aylan," he said with a tired weariness, "I have a story to tell you."

Once, the universe must have been young, an emptiness filled with fiery gases and slowly-spinning new-born suns. And even then, the Player must have been preparing the Board for his game.

Milenn first saw the light of day on a smoking, roaring world of shaggy beast-men and thudding hairy animals. It was a world on the Rim of the Galaxy, with a feeble yellow star and a single pock-marked moon.

It was the only world that ever produced sentient life, and its children were destined to seed the Galaxy.

For the Game. For the Player's inscrutable purpose.

Milenn, the shaggy beast-man, possessed no more than the limited awareness of his fellows. Later, though, they called him Prometheus. He did not discover fire, but as elder of his tribe he saved from death the man who did. He caused a priesthood to be set up, and his tribe worshipped fire, and conquered their world.

And he was punished with eternal life, to come again and again as a child and to remember and to die and to come again. . . . Of course, he learned. Memories of his previous life returned to him at puberty, and each life wrote new wonders on the tablet of experience. For a time he rebelled. He refused to be the Player's instrument, refused to pass his knowledge on. And there was no retribution, save in his soul. He could not live with the sloughing beasts he was born among. Frantically, he tried the life of the hermit, and he was driven back by loneliness to human companionship.

So, finally, he became the Civilizer.

He was Gilgamesh, Odin, Ra, Indra, Zeus, Tonactechtli, Moses, Gandhi, Hammarskjöld, Holden-Smith, Porter, and Andreas. In the mud of the Nile he trod water and straw; his statue was carried before the tallow candles in Tenochtitlan; he advised the Great One in Tibet while the wind whistled through his thin bones; he thundered in the Terran Planetary Parliament; he laboured on alien worlds, muscles twisting to hammer wood and steel into homes for his fellows. And everywhere, he remembered. Peace was his goal, for no man can go through a million years' odyssey without learning compassion and humanity.

"The years have fled," Milenn said quietly, "and I have lived as your grandfather Yusten, as an adviser to the Monarch of Kiel, as a singer of ballads in the halls of Blucher, and now I am your friend, you who are about to bring about the widespread peace I have laboured aeons to achieve. And I am afraid of the Player."

In the great garden that was Prima, the birds continued their singing unconcernedly, and a gentle breeze tossed the leaves and grasses as it had done for centuries, but the breath of age was strong now, an age greater than the ancient Council Hall below, greater than the dreams of men. Milenn stood with his friends in the quiet afternoon, strong, young, and his mind encompassed a universe of history.

Aylan's eyes were focused on a horizon beyond the azure sky of Prima, and when he turned to Milenn his face was shining with a great vision. He took Adriel's hand, and said in a strange forced voice, "Come. We have destiny to meet."

The grav-tube was waiting, and the three floated gently down towards the Council Hall.

In the vast hall sat the rulers and representatives of the Galaxy. They were restless, waiting to hear the terms desired by the young Emperor whose father had conquered them. Aylan looked at their faces and there was resentment and bitterness everywhere. These were men beaten by virtue of Loren's technological strength—there was no lack of spirit among them. The Emperor was glad, for he wanted strong men, capable men with the vision to see beyond their own pettiness.

The three were the last to enter the Hall. Bitter the conquered leaders might be, but they had no wish to antagonize their new master. Aylan squeezed Adriel's cool lovely hand, and when he rose to speak there was silence throughout the hall.

"My friends," he began. There was a discernible brightening of some of the faces—a hostile dictator would hardly call his victims "friends". "Although you are unaware of the fact, the capital planets of your systems were almost nova-bombed by my forces less than a week ago."

He paused, and glanced sideways at Adriel. Her eyes were closed, and he could feel the waves of apprehension she was directing out into the audience before him.

"My commander of forces mutinied against Loren and was endeavouring to set himself up as Emperor. At personal danger to myself, I took a fleet out and destroyed him and sixty of my own naval vessels."

Puzzlement, dawning awareness. Aylan's head was held high, and his words were intense, his eyes bright.

"I did this because I had your interests at heart. I could easily have been killed, but I considered the risk worth taking if I could in this way convince you that I am not seeking my own aggrandizement." A wave of relief, and a warmth towards the young man before them. Adriel did not have to engender the emotion; she merely intensified it.

Aylan's speech had been semantically designed to elicit the desired emotional response from the audience. Beside him, the beautiful Emote sent wave after crashing wave of complementary emotion out into the Hall, judging, balancing, dancing in an emotional control that was practically instinctive. They were on the edges of their chairs now, breathing the glory of the vision Aylan was painting. Memories fled through Aylan's mind: childhood days, talking to Milenn, nights of anguished mental conflict, the evening at Nara with the Galactic Lens burning around him and Milenn's words setting his mind on fire with a towering hope for the future. And now, in the huge ancient Hall, the leaders of the Galaxy were sharing this dream, guided by his words and the Emotive control of a slim lovely girl.

Finally, Aylan was silent, and Adriel played a last crashing crescendo of trust, enthusiasm, and accord. Without prompting, the audience who half an hour before had stared with bitter, angry eyes at the young Emperor rose to their feet in wild applause. Their shout was a mighty *Fiat* to peace, a cry that rocked the walls. . . .

Literally. Milenn came to his feet, and the terror was black on him again. In numb horror he saw the walls of the Council Hall fold in like a freckled banana, and the roof gaped wide as the whole planet seemed to peel open. Around him, the other figures of the Game screamed and ran amok, tearing, howling like animals. The noise somehow faded away, and the ruined planet bubbled with spurting boiling magma that ran around Milenn but could not touch him. He realized that he was screaming too, for the stars were whirling in a mad kaleidoscope of light and they were falling on him, globes of roaring fire, tiny marbles of cold luminescence, a spraying spiral of light. He was huge beyond belief, the pinpoints of light were stars, galaxies, and the universe was fading, eddying, insubstantial, and he was screaming at the Player why, why, why. . . ?

Alone. Darkness, bodiless, infinite. All the questions answered and the tears wept. The Immortal wondered at the memory, and knew the reason. There was no Player. There was only himself, alone, eternally lonely. Infinity is a quiet place, eternity a lonely time. The Immortal remembered himself as Milenn, and forever the memory satisfied him. But forever is a short while, and memory is no cure for loneliness. Only participation, and forgetfulness.

The Tasks had been a good idea, but they had ended. The problem he had set himself: a universe, a race of naturally belligerent sapients, a goal of peace, freely accepted by them. And three times he had succeeded. Planetary government, Galactic empire, Galactic Federation. Himself eternal, not knowing the reason, only aware of the compulsion.

An Immortal Child grows lonely in the dark of eternity, and he knew that there was forgetfulness in the Game. So again in the deep of himself he uttered the Words.

"Let there be light!"

And, yet again, there was light.